"I did it, Judie," Tack screamed over the phone.

"Not so loud." Judie covered her ear. "Now what did you say?"

"I got a date with Sara Fielder," he said proudly.

Judie felt oddly unhappy, but said, "Great, Tack. How'd it happen?"

Tack told her he had bumped into Sara in the grocery store. "We talked for a while, then I asked her what she was doing, and bingo!"

There was a silence, then Tack asked: "Aren't you proud of me?"

"I think it's terrific," Judie said emptily.

"Is something wrong, Judie?"

"No, crazy, I'm just in a funny mood." Judie feigned excitement and then made an excuse to hang up. Suddenly she began to cry. She felt worse knowing she didn't really have a reason to. Her best friend had a date with "the girl of his dreams" and she was crying. Judie felt guilty, but she couldn't help thinking that if Tack and Sara got along, she'd see less and less of him.

"Think about basketball," Judie told herself. "Better yet, go practice."

OUT OF BOUNDS

by

Lori Boatright

FAWCETT JUNIPER • NEW YORK

A Fawcett Juniper Book

Published by Ballantine Books

Copyright © 1982 by Lori Boatright

ISBN 0-449-70028-3

Manufactured in the United States of America

First Ballantine Books Edition: July 1982
10 9 8 7 6 5 4 3 2 1

FOR BRUCE—

who took the blame when I broke the porch light that night Dad said it was too cold and too dark to play.

Chapter One

"You don't have any idea what you're getting into."
Cassie sighed. "Don't say you weren't warned...."

Judie shrugged her shoulders, gripped her gym bag
tightly, and mumbled good-bye to her friend. Then she
walked slowly toward the locker room door. Inside, the
room smelled like locker rooms everywhere, but the
showers, benches, and stray towels were foreign—this
wasn't her locker room. As Judie lowered her gym bag
onto one of the benches, she searched in vain for a light
switch. There wasn't even anyone around to ask.

Back at Bookner, things had been different. Sure,
she dressed in a separate room there, too, but the guys
would yell and joke with her, and pound on the door
as they passed. Every time she finished dressing, either
Mark or Jeff would be waiting for her. If she took too
long, they'd yell for her to hurry up. Now she had to
prove herself all over again. The boy's varsity. Her
stomach turned somersaults just thinking about it.

As Judie sat down on the cold bench and opened her
bag with its Bookner Bluejay emblem on the side, she
longed for her old high school. She'd gotten a letter
from Mark that weekend, telling her how the old team
had already had tryouts, and how much they could use
her. While Judie pulled on her favorite blue T-shirt
and put the finishing touches on the bows of her bas-

ketball sneakers, she wondered if instead she should be putting her clothes back on—and going home.

She recalled her conversation with Coach Arthur this morning, when she tried to tell him about her plans to try out. He had stared at her for several seconds, completely incredulous, then he spoke. "You're a smart girl, Judie. I'll respect whatever you decide."

Judie's strained expression relaxed a little as the coach walked away, until he suddenly turned back and placed his hand on her shoulder. He faced her directly, probing her deep blue eyes with his firm brown ones.

"Don't forget Meier High is a lot bigger than your old school, Judie. Competition is really stiff. Maybe you ought to think more seriously about the girl's team....Mrs. Forster is a great coach."

The familiar squeak of new sneakers on the freshly waxed gym floor interrupted Judie's thoughts. She told herself to relax. She was a good ball player. She could handle opposition. As she paced around the room, trying to build her confidence, she thought once more about going home. If she were at Bookner, Mark or Jeff would be pounding on her door by now. But this wasn't Bookner; it was Meier High. And she'd have to deal with that. Judie resolutely took a deep breath and sauntered through the swinging doors. "It's too late now, kid," she scolded herself, walking out onto the shiny court, "you're on!"

Basketballs bounced and rolled all around the floor, and several pairs of hands grabbed and tugged at each. One bounced right to her and as she sank her first basket, the boys began to stare. No more shots were attempted; the dribbling stopped, too. Only Judie continued, afraid to stop and explain her presence for fear she'd look uneasy. She tried to ignore the laughter and the whispered comments. One voice, though, rose above the sound of her basketball. "What the hell do you think you're doing? This is boys' tryout session, not girls'. Varsity basketball."

She stopped, finally, and looked over at the tall, dark, curly haired boy who had spoken. "I know that," she said softly. She put up another shot, but her nerves got the best of her, and it missed the entire backboard and went into the bleachers.

"Nice shot," the same voice rang out, and everyone laughed. Judie knew that she should laugh, too, to ease the tension a little, but she just couldn't. She wanted to scream out that she'd played some varsity ball as a sophomore, that she'd been named All-Conference Honorable Mention along with two senior guards, but she knew it would only make things worse. Telling them would never do, and so far she wasn't doing such a good job of showing them. If only one of them would smile at her, give her some sign that she was okay, or if Mark or Jeff would walk through the door and tell this clown that he was dead wrong. She knew she could play with them, but damned if it didn't hurt that none of them knew it.

Coach Arthur blew his whistle from the opposite corner of the gym. "Hustle over," he roared, clapping his hands, "and move! Move! Move!"

Judie kept up with the group, and as the coach began his spiel about the upcoming season, she surveyed the players standing around her. She breathed a little easier when she realized she wasn't the shortest player, though being 5'9" definitely restricted her to playing guard. Back at Bookner, she had started the season playing back-up guard for the varsity. She spent her freshman year on the girls' team, but, when she was named All State, the boys' coach recruited her to the boys' squad. Her brother had played for Coach Mickes the year before, and she liked the way the man coached. She missed being the brightest star on the girls' team, but she liked the thrill of better competition, too.

But Meier High was different. No one begged her to try out; no one wanted her here now. She forced her attention back to Coach Arthur's lecture when she heard him say, "Everyone will get a fair shake. I counted thirty-six heads, and I'll keep twenty-five. You seniors haven't secured yourselves a position just because you're seniors or because you've played for me before, contrary to popular belief. You sophomores and juniors are going to have to boot the older guys out to make a spot for yourselves. I don't play favorites, and I ask you to remember that *no nonsense will be tolerated.*" He bounced the basketball emphatically, then looked back up into the crowd of eager faces. "We'll practice every day this week from three thirty to six. Next Monday, I'll post the team roster outside my office. Remember one thing: I expect you to go by the school rules from now on. No drinking, smoking, or late-night partying. At all times you are to behave like gentlemen."

The curly haired boy laughed softly, and when the coach realized why, he added, "Or ladies, whatever the case may be." Judie knew her face was red.

"Ten laps around the gym and begin lay-up formation," Coach Arthur yelled. Then he blew his shrill whistle once more; the competition was on.

Chapter Two

By Wednesday, Judie knew who definitely would make the team and who definitely would not. Grayson Griffin and Phil Derrick, both senior returning lettermen, were shoo-ins. But guys like Billy Wales and Ted Bonebark might as well hang up their sneakers right now. Judie played better each day, but she wasn't certain about her standing within the group.

There were more talented ball players at Meier than at Bookner, but then again, the school was a lot bigger. She had even made a few friends in the past few days. Charlie Sloan and Tack Cienelli treated her great: just like one of the guys.

Unfortunately, Franky Warnik, the curly haired boy who gave her trouble the first day, was keeping up his harassment. Some of the guys he hung around gave her trouble, too—especially Steve Merrill. One day, when she made a stupid mistake in a scrimmage, Franky smarted off under his breath like always, but Grayson Griffin came to her defense. "Give her a break, Warnik," he said simply. People like Griffin, Derrick, and Boyd Abbott, the best junior player, were well respected and could say whatever they liked. They never let anyone forget that someday this bunch of competitors would become a single unit: the team.

By Friday, the tension was stifling. Judie and Tack talked during lunch about how the tall guys had it made. Pete Dalton, a lanky 6'7" sophomore, would make the team from his height alone, and he acted accordingly. He knew that he was going to be the reserve center and, short of a disaster or a miracle, there was no way he could edge out Anthony Northe, a stockier 6'6" junior, or lose his position, as no one else broke 6'5" except Abbott, who was a natural-born forward. Tack laughed when Judie complained about the unfairness.

"Why are you laughing, jerk? You're only a couple of inches taller than I am."

"You keep griping, but what you don't realize is that the other guys are probably complaining about both of us, too," he said.

"What?" Judie asked, momentarily perplexed. She didn't follow.

Tack used a falsetto voice, "That lousy Judie's going to make it because she's a girl, and the coach feels sorry for her. And that creep Tack will make it because his brother Seth was a big hot-shot player three years ago." They both laughed.

"You're probably right," she said, shaking her strawberry blond hair in irritation.

About that time, Franky Warnik and Steve Merrill walked up to their table. "Tonight's our last shot, so to speak," Franky said in a cocky voice.

"So to speak," Tack said.

"Think you're ready, Conklin?" Franky asked Judie toughly.

"Ready as ever, I guess," she answered.

"How about you, Franky? Ready to burn up the track?" Tack asked, smiling broadly.

"Whatever," he said, not used to being the one getting teased. "I figure I'm in, and Steve here is in." He began rubbing his chin, and the sparkle came back to

12

his eye. "Naturally, Abbott and Derrick are in," he continued, "and Lord Grayson Griffin Our Saviour is in. And Conklin here is in just because Coach Arthur has a soft spot in his heart."

"And he likes leggy blondes," Steve added, obviously repeating a line of Franky's.

Tack stood up. "Take it back, idiot," he said coolly.

Franky moved in closer and said softly, "I knew there was some reason you've been hanging around her, Cienelli." He paused for effect, then said even more quietly, "You like her legs, too."

Tack pushed Franky against the cafeteria wall, and Judie didn't know quite what to do. "Look, smart ass," Tack said, "you apologize." Tack held him by the shirt collar, and he had pinned him in under the P.A. system. A crowd was beginning to gather, and Judie knew she had to react.

"Knock it off, Tack," she said, walking over to them. "It's not your battle; it's mine." No one moved. Judie was breathing hard when she said, "I said let him go. If it was your fight you could do whatever you pleased. I'm certainly not defending Franky, but it's my fight. So let him go."

She watched Tack closely as he made up his mind. Slowly, as he let go of Franky, the muscles in his back began to loosen. Once Franky was standing by himself, Tack patronizingly smoothed Franky's shirt and pretended to dust it off. Though Franky was slightly taller than Tack, Tack's frame was stronger, and there was fear in Franky's eyes.

When Franky regained his composure, he motioned for Steve to follow him to the cafeteria door. Before the lunch crowd had gone back to their food, Franky yelled, "Does she cut up your meat, too, Cienelli?" Franky and Steve laughed loudly and walked out, not giving Tack

13

a chance to respond. And when Tack turned around, Judie could tell he was angry with her.

"Why'd you make me quit? I was going to bust that creep's head," Tack said. He refused to look straight at her, and when their eyes did meet, Tack's soft blue eyes were icy.

Judie leaned closer to Tack and said, "I don't want to mess up your chances for the team. And besides, if we're going to be friends, you'll have to understand that I will handle my troubles in my own way. I may be a girl, but that doesn't mean I'm helpless." She looked at Tack earnestly, but he turned away.

She grabbed his arm. "Tack, I understand what you were trying to do, and I appreciate it. I'm not asking you to change your ways. You're going to get flack just for being my friend, but you're not my guardian angel, okay?" He still didn't answer. Judie tried the only other thing she could think of. "Besides, Tack," she teased, "you were just venting your frustration on poor Franky. There's no need for that. You know we'll both make the team what with my being a girl and your having a hot-shot brother."

Finally, he laughed. "Okay, but I still wish I could've busted his head a little. It might have been your battle, but it was my ass on the line in front of that crowd."

"You know, Tack," Judie said disgustedly, "you act a lot like everybody else sometimes." She started walking to class.

"I'm just trying to take away Franky's spot on the team."

Judie stopped, then looked back to clear her confusion.

"You know he'll make the team solely on the grounds that he's the most obnoxious."

Judie chuckled, then began walking again. She wondered how she would've reacted had she been in Tack's position.

Later that day, the group of hopefuls shot baskets and warmed up without the usual joking and kidding around. Only the most talented players talked, and when the coach came out, the action froze.

"Okay," he said, "I want to see the following ten on the floor. Griffin, Merrill, Northe, Abbott, and Conklin, and then Warnik, Nisbett, Dalton, Derrick, and Wales. Shirts and skins. Let's go." He blew his whistle.

The named ten ran out to position, except Franky, who stood on the sidelines, scratching his head. "Who's shirts and who's skins?" he asked, winking at Steve Merrill.

"You know something, Warnik? Your joke is getting old." The coach turned around to get his clipboard, leaving Franky mid-joke, and Judie felt slightly triumphant. Franky ran to position, and the coach shouted, "Play ball!"

Judie was nervous. She noticed that there was some sort of strategy in how the coach had them playing against each other. What bothered her most was that she was set against Billy Wales, a terrible sophomore guard. Shake it off, she told herself, and make it count.

She took the ball away from him during the first play, and she fed it downcourt to Grayson Griffin for an easy basket. In the first few minutes, shirts had a six-point lead, and the gap grew. Judie made a shot from the top of the key and one of two foul shots. She felt better about the assists, and she even pulled down a rebound. Shortly, Coach Arthur blew his whistle.

"Wales and Nisbett, sit down. Connors and Danschenko, go in for them."

Judie felt good; she knew that to be put out so soon would be a bad indication. She had more trouble with

Bruce Connors, but she held her own. He outweighed her a good deal, but she was quicker and could fast-break on him easily. In just a few minutes, the coach replaced all ten of them with a new group. On his way out to play, Tack grabbed Judie and said, "Good job, kid."

"Thanks, Tack," she said, "and good luck to you." Judie rooted for him silently on the sidelines. Charlie Sloan was playing forward, but he wasn't doing very well. Judie felt uneasy; poor Charlie was already way down her imaginary competitors list. Tack was playing well; Judie thought he might end up playing second-string varsity or start on the B team. Either way, he had nothing to worry about.

The practice session ended early—about five o'clock—they didn't have to run laps. The coach called them over to a corner of the court before letting them go.

"Like I said earlier, the team roster will be posted outside my office on Monday morning. Eleven of you will not be on that list. If you'd like to talk to me after the posting, I'll be there during lunch. Monday afternoon, twenty-five of you are to be dressed out, ready to practice at three thirty." He started to blow his whistle, but stopped, then added, "And before I forget, thanks to all of you for trying out."

The players were quiet as they walked to the dressing rooms. Judie wished that there was at least one more girl trying out for the team. The empty locker room ritual made her feel like some sort of alien. While the boys were sweating it out together, Judie was all alone.

Chapter Three

The weekend was long and dull. Judie spent Saturday afternoon at her girlfriend Cassie's house, but she really wanted to call Tack. At school, it was natural for them to get together, but today, at home, she just couldn't bring herself to call him. For one thing, her mother would kill her, but that wasn't all of it. It scared her—what if it messed up their friendship? What if his father answered? She resigned herself to not talking to him, but she still felt terribly deprived. Cassie mentioned Tack once that day, too, but her question shocked Judie. "Are you guys dating?"

"Dating?" Judie protested, "are you kidding? We're just good friends."

"Whatever you say," Cassie said, her dark brown eyes flashing, her lips curving into a knowing smile.

Not long after that, Judie made a feeble excuse about homework and left. She was a little angry with Cassie for not understanding that she and Tack were just friends. Cassie should know better. As Judie pulled her car out of the driveway, and realized that she didn't want to go home yet. She wanted some time for herself, so she drove to McDonald's to get some tea.

As she walked into the restaurant, she saw Russ Dwyer and Boyd Abbott in the rear of the store. Both guys were good players, though Boyd was better. Russ was a steady player, he had good hands and could feed

Anthony Northe in the inside about as well as anyone. Because Russ wasn't flashy, Judie, like everyone else, hadn't noticed him much until late in the first week of practice. He wasn't a high scorer and didn't draw much attention to himself. Personally, he was much the same: quiet and shy, but nice. Boyd was just the opposite—not only a high-scoring forward, but outgoing and popular. Judie hid her smile as she approached them, but she couldn't help thinking that Russ was the better looking one of the two despite Boyd's popularity. Russ was dark, had wavy black hair and eyes so brown that Judie had to force herself not to stare into them. Her eyes just locked into his whenever she looked at him. She was a little self-conscious about how it must appear to him. She was glad she had changed clothes. before going to Cassie's that afternoon.

"Hey Judie," Boyd yelled across the restaurant. "Ready for Monday?"

"Who is?" she yelled back. They both laughed, and Boyd motioned her over. Boyd was tall, always wore nice tailored clothes, and seemed older. Judie always felt immature when she talked to him.

"Pull up a plastic booth," he said. Judie was grateful. Anytime any of the players were genuinely friendly, she thought more of them. And Boyd was so popular that it seemed especially good of him—he had no reason to be good to her. He just was. "Russ and I were talking," he said while munching on a hamburger, "and we think you'll make it. And Tack will make it." He shook his head up and down like a judge handing down a decision. Everything he said came out with a certainty that Judie envied.

"Do you really think so?" she asked. "Everybody knows you'll make it, Boyd. Everybody thinks so." She silently cursed herself for rambling on so. "I'm sure you'll make it, too, Russ. You're good."

"He might be a shoo-in," Russ said, pointing to Boyd, "but I'm worried."

"You guys worry too much," Boyd said in his pompous but charming way. "Okay, sure, I'll make the team easy enough. But I want to start for the varsity, and I may not get to. As for you two, you'll see that the coach knows you've got talent. You'll both make it, so quit worrying."

"I hope so," Judie said. Russ nodded a "me, too." They talked about their predictions, about both the team and the season. When she was leaving, Judie felt good.

"See you later, Judie," Russ yelled.

"Take care," Boyd added.

Judie waved. They were all right.

Monday morning Judie convinced her parents that she should drive rather than ride the bus. She was breathing hard when she told her mom that she didn't know what time she'd be home. Either three thirty or six—one or the other. Her mother simply sighed.

Judie's dad never gave her any trouble about playing on the boys' team. In fact, he enjoyed following her team back in Iowa. And though he never said anything, Judie thought that he was proud of her for trying out for the Bookner team. Judie's mother was another story. She wished Judie had been a cheerleader instead of a ballplayer, although she usually had the sense to keep her opinion to herself.

As Judie finished dressing, she looked at herself in the mirror. She needed to gain a little weight—her jeans were a little baggier around the middle than usual. Her mom complained about her wearing jeans so often, but Judie felt uncomfortable in dresses. She liked to be able

19

to sit any way she wanted, and besides, she always managed to get runs in her nylons no matter how short a period of time she wore them. And today, especially, she had no time to worry about runs in her nylons.

Tack was pulling into the student parking lot as Judie was getting out of her car. She waited for him so they could check the roster together.

"This is the earliest I've been to school in a while," Tack said, pausing to think. "I guess since this time last year." They both laughed nervous laughs and quickened their pace.

There was a crowd around the small bulletin board, and Judie and Tack had to push and shove just to see it. Judie shut her eyes for a moment, took a deep breath, and looked up at the single typewritten sheet on the board. It read:

MEIER MAVERICKS BASKETBALL ROSTER:

Abbott, Boyd	Merrill, Steve
Brondel, Marty	Miner, Danny
Cienelli, Tack	Northe, Anthony
Conklin, Judie	Regan, Blair
Connors, Bruce	Shackett, David
Dale, Mike	Spencer, Ryan
Dalton, Pete	Suchinski, Mark
Danschenko, Nick	Wallach, Michael
Derrick, Phil	Walters, Don
Dwyer, Russ	Warner, Kenneth
Griffin, Grayson	Warnik, Franky
Hickman, Milt	Young, Turner
Lay, Rocky	

Judie's heart was beating fast and Tack grabbed her

and hugged her. She felt terrific. "We made it!" she yelled.

Just then, Charlie Sloan walked up to the crowd. "Hey, Tack, can you see it from there? The list, I mean," he yelled. Tack looked at Judie, then back at Charlie. Tack nodded. He glanced back at the roster to make sure he hadn't just overlooked Charlie's name.

"Well, did I make it?" Charlie asked anxiously.

Tack swallowed hard, then said softly, "No, Charlie, not this time. Sorry." Judie couldn't stand to look at Charlie, and she felt bad for yelling the minute before.

"Did you guys make it?" he asked.

"Uh-huh," Judie heard herself say. Tack nodded.

"Congratulations to you both," he said dully as he tightened his grip on his gym bag and turned to walk away.

"Let's get out of here," Tack said, "before we have to witness more casualties." They were silent as they walked out the door and back out to the parking lot to wait for the first bell. Tack offered her his hand, and she shook it. "Congratulations, Judie. I think you're really brave."

"Brave?"

"Yeah. For sticking it out. A lot of guys wouldn't have."

"Thanks, Tack. Not just for the compliment, but for being my friend, too."

"Don't get sappy," he said, getting off the hood of his car, his face red. "I didn't say you were ready for the varsity or anything."

As they talked about the team—who made it and who didn't—and their goals, Judie often wanted to say more. Suddenly Tack interrupted their conversation and pointed toward the hilltop where cars always crested going a little too fast. The blazing autumn colors of the trees on the hill were overwhelming, and Judie was a little shaken by the beauty of the moment. She took a deep breath, then turned to Tack, who was staring at her.

"It's a pretty time of year," he murmured. Judie simply nodded.

The spell was broken however, when they started walking toward the building—Franky Warnik pulled into the parking lot.

"Did *he* make it?" Tack asked Judie.

"Of course," Judie replied gingerly. "As a result, it's going to be a lovely season!"

Chapter Four

Basketball practice that afternoon was very different from tryouts. There was a new atmosphere, but the competitive feelings had not disappeared. The team had been chosen, but the varsity/B team line had not yet been drawn.

Judie didn't recognize all the names on the list that morning, but now the faces were all familiar. She'd worry about assigning names to the faces later. Right now she had to worry about playing well: her free-throw percentage needed drastic improvement. It was harder when everyone was looking only at her. Somehow, the pressure wasn't as bad when there were nine others on the court. Shooting free throws made Judie think that the others were all waiting for "the girl" to mess up.

The whistle sounded, and Coach Arthur directed, "Lay-ups. Let's go!" Franky got in line behind Judie.

"Congratulations, Franky," she said, hoping to bury the ax now that they were teammates.

"Well, you, too," he said, oddly sincere. Steve Merrill got in line behind Franky, and Franky quickly added, "But after all, how could the coach resist the Wonder Woman of Meier High?"

"Yeah," Steve said, following the gist of the conversation. "The team's ratings might drop." They both laughed more loudly than the joke was worth.

"You guys are just too much for little old me to keep

up with," Judie said sarcastically as she approached the front of the line. Bruce Connors fed her the ball perfectly, and she knew her form was good as she backboarded the ball for the basket.

Later that afternoon during a scrimmage, Judie tripped over Mike Dale's foot, and she turned her ankle slightly. She made a special effort not to complain too much, afraid she'd be branded a "wimpy girl" for life. Tack noticed that she was in pain, and as soon as the coach substituted someone in for her, Tack sat her down and wrapped her ankle. "Make sure not to whine or anything," he said, looking up at her.

"I know," she said, happy to have her strategy confirmed. "Tack, you're okay, you know?" He smiled and returned to his seat on the bench. The next substitution was for him.

Judie watched the boys more intently than usual. Griffin was an extraordinary shot. His height didn't hurt either; college scouts would remember him. She leaned over to Russ Dwyer and asked, "How long has Griffin been a starter here?"

"Since my freshman year. His sophomore year. He's something else, huh?"

"Yeah," she said as he swished another one from the top of the key.

When she was younger, Judie dreamed of being a famous basketball player. In fact, when people asked her what she wanted to be when she grew up, she always answered seriously, "A Harlem Globetrotter," only to be met with much laughter and pleas to repeat it for Aunt Martha or Uncle Dick. She learned soon enough that Uncle Dick and Aunt Martha no longer thought the subject funny; they thought it was ridiculous.

"Nonsense," her mother would say when her father

wasn't home. "A girl's got no business playing basketball." As Judie sat watching Grayson Griffin, she wondered how his dreams were regarded when he was younger. Did the grown-ups laugh at him, too? Did they try to keep him from practicing? "They probably didn't try to put him in a tutu," she said aloud, thinking of her mother's disastrous attempt to make her into a ballerina.

"What?" Russ asked, his face contorted in a frown.

"Nothing," Judie said, embarrassed for talking to herself. "I was just thinking of the time my mom, well, never mind." Her voice trailed off as her face got redder.

Russ's face softened. "Really, I mean it. What were you saying?"

Judie hesitantly explained how her mother had enrolled her in her first dance class. "I had two left feet to begin with," she said, "and those toe slippers felt really crummy. I couldn't wait to pull them off when I got home so I could put on my basketball shoes. And there was this one girl in our class who was worse than I was. Audrey somebody. Well, the teacher couldn't stand Audrey, and Audrey wasn't too crazy about her either. Once, during my first day, Audrey was getting yelled at, but not just about her dancing. Audrey liked to dance in her leotards, but there was a rule that you had to wear a tutu. Anyway, the teacher told her to go put on her tutu..."

"What's a tutu?"

"That ruffly thing that goes around your waist."

"Okay, now I've got it."

"Anyway," Judie continued, "when she came out of the dressing room, Audrey had the tutu on her head."

Russ laughed. "Really? On her head?"

"Yeah," Judie said, starting to laugh, too. "And we were only about eight years old. Well, the next week

25

or so was the recital for the kids who'd been there a while, and Audrey was one of the dancers. During this one solo dance, all the chorus dancers had to go backstage and change into blue tutus. One by one, the dancers came back onstage, and when it was Audrey's turn, out she came with her tutu on her head. The whole audience cracked up. I mean here was this formal, suit-and-tie kind of thing, and out walks this skinny little eight-year-old who steals the show. It was great."

Russ was laughing with Judie, but he looked confused. "So what does this have to do with Grayson?"

"Well," Judie said thoughtfully, "they ended up kicking Audrey out of class, so I told Mom I wanted to quit, but she wouldn't let me. I went for a while longer, but finally she let me quit when I hinted at what *I* was planning for my first recital. But she was really mad at me, just the same."

"And Grayson?" Russ asked again.

"He probably never had anything like that happen to him," Judie said. She knew she wasn't making much sense, but she didn't know how to correct it.

"Judie," he said after pausing to think, "you might be a good ball player, but your punch lines need work."

She shrugged and he laughed. For the first time, Judie noticed that Russ had dimples and that when he laughed he looked like a little boy—a high contrast to the normally serious, intense manner that had initially attracted her to him.

Before it was time for the showers, Coach Arthur called the team together for what Judie called the big "all for one and one for all" lecture. Judie thought he looked at Franky a bit more than the other players, but she couldn't be certain. She had trouble giving the coach her full attention; she'd heard the same lecture at Bookner. One unexpected turn in the lecture how-ever, managed to surprise her.

"This season marks the first time Meier's ever had a young lady playing for the boys' team. As you know, Judie's a good player and that is why she's here. I expect you to treat her accordingly. She's, well," he said, rub-bing his chin, trying to think of the right words, "she's one of us."

After the team ran laps, they headed for the showers. Back in the locker room, Judie laughed to herself about being "one of the boys." She unfastened the barrette that kept her long strawberry blond hair out of her face while she played, and she brushed out her hair before showering. Judie kept a blow dryer in her locker, and Tack ribbed her about being so vain.

"It's not vanity," she told him one afternoon after he'd kidded her. "It'd be insane to go out with wet hair in this weather. My hair doesn't dry as fast as yours." Even when she explained, he didn't quit teasing her, but Judie didn't mind. It felt good to be teased a little.

As Judie reached for the door on her way out of the gym, Marty Brondel, a sophomore forward, ran ahead of her to open it for her, and he stood there, smiling sweetly, as he waited for her to go through. Easy does it, she told herself.

"Thanks, Marty," she said as she walked through. Then she pushed open the outer door and held it open for him, not letting it shut until he walked through.

"Thanks," he said finally, somewhat confused, as the cold October wind slapped his face.

Chapter Five

"You got a letter from Jeff today," Judie's mother said as she stirred the gravy.

"Really? Where is it?"

"On the coffee table, I think."

Judie got three plates out of the cabinet and put them on the table. "Well, aren't you going to see what it says?"

"Yeah, sure," Judie replied, walking over to get it. Jeff Burk had been her official boyfriend at Bookner. Mrs. Burk and Judie's mom had gone to school together, and they pushed the two kids together a little more than Judie liked. It wasn't that she didn't like Jeff; she did. In fact, it was sort of a good arrangement because Judie felt nervous dating other boys. If she had a boyfriend, she would have to worry about the pressure to have sex. Jeff was nice and sweet and safe: convenient. But Judie never enjoyed kissing Jeff—it was like kissing a cousin or one of her brother's buddies she'd known since grade school.

Jeff's letter was nice, as usual. He said he hoped she could come back for homecoming so they could go to the game and to the dance together. He said he missed her. Judie wondered if he missed her like parted lovers in the old World War II movies, or if he missed her like she missed him—like a friend. Not being around Jeff was like not being around Mark and like not being around Jean. It wasn't a throb, just an occasional pang.

"What does he say?" her mother asked.

"Oh, not much," Judie said, folding up the letter and stuffing it in her back jeans pocket. "The football team lost to Patterson, and Rick Smiley was in a car accident," she called to her mom. Don't mention the homecoming invitation, she thought.

"Was he hurt?"

"Broke his collarbone," Judie answered. She hated discussing Jeff's letters with her mom.

"When is Jeff coming to see you?" her mom asked innocently.

Judie noted the "you" instead of an "us," and the usage irritated her. "I don't know, Mom.... But Rick ran a stop light. Jeff says Rick's dad won't let him use the car for a while."

"Maybe he can come around homecoming," Mrs. Conklin continued.

Judie knew her mom was still talking about Jeff's visit, but she said, "No, I think Mr. Smiley's thinking more along the lines of Thanksgiving."

Her mom gave her a quizzical look. "What does Mr. Smiley have to do with Jeff?" she asked.

"Not much, I imagine," Judie answered. "Rick has more to do with Jeff than Mr. Smiley does. More compatible, I would say." Judie knew she was really pushing her luck, so she went into the bathroom and shut the door.

"Judie, what are you talking about?" her mother yelled, irritated.

"Can't hear you, Mom," Judie answered as she turned on the faucet. She couldn't please her mom all the time, she reflected. When enough time had passed,

Judie went back to the kitchen and ate dinner with her parents, no questions asked.

"Tack's coming over tomorrow night," Judie said off-handedly.

"Is he the curly haired one? The tall one?" her father asked, trying to place him from the one scrimmage he'd seen.

"No, Dad, you're thinking of Franky," Judie said, disgusted.

"Franky's the obnoxious one from the stories, dear. Don't you remember?" Rose Conklin said, winking at her husband.

"Oh, yeah," he said, remembering several stories. "So which one's Tack?"

"You know, Dad, the guard who played opposite Griffin for a while. Blonde, blue-eyed. Had on a Genesis concert T-shirt."

"Good hook shot?"

"That's him," she answered. "He's going to pick me up in a few minutes, too. We're going to the Recreation Center for a pick-up game."

Her mother looked forlorn. Her father recognized the look and then leaned over and whispered, "It's a basketball phrase, dear. They're just going to round up some kids for a game."

"Oh, I see," she said, clearing the table of the dirty dishes while Judie went to her room to change.

Tack honked loudly for Judie to come out. She knew that that wouldn't go over too well with her parents, so she hurried out to meet him before they could protest.

"I'll be home by ten," she said, shutting the door behind her. She slid into the passenger side of the beat-up blue Mustang Tack inherited from his brother Seth who inherited it from his brother Chris.

"Watch that spring," he cautioned, indicating the exposed spring in the torn upholstery. "It sticks through."

"Oh, I don't know," Judie teased, "it might be fun." As soon as she'd said it, she felt awkward. Tack laughed, but they both remained unusually silent as they drove across town.

Right before reaching the Center, Tack asked, "Do girls think about it as much as guys do?"

Judie thought for a moment, then answered, "I don't know. Maybe."

"I think about it a lot," he said, getting more embarrassed with each word. He found a parking space and wheeled in. As they were walking toward the building, Judie wanted to tell him that she thought about sex a lot, whether all girls did or not. But she was too afraid to let Tack know. She felt so ignorant about sex; boys always seemed to know all about it. She couldn't help remembering the crude jokes from junior high; the memories kept her lips sealed.

There were a few players warming up when they got inside. Marge Fielder was one of them. Judie wanted to get to know Marge better; she was a star player on the girls' team. Sometimes Judie felt as though she'd let the girls' team down, or that they thought she thought she was better than they were.

"Hey, Marge," Tack yelled, "want to play some three on three?" indicating Judie, three guys, and himself.

"Sure, I'm game," Marge responded.

Marge was a good ball handler, and as she brought the ball downcourt, Judie could tell she was being tested. Several times, Marge tried to maneuver around Judie to make her look foolish. Then, after passing off and getting the ball back, Marge once again tried some fancy dribbling to get away from Judie, but Judie forcefully took the ball away from her and scored easily.

As the game progressed, Judie could tell Marge was beginning to respect her kind of playing, even though Marge's team eventually won.

"Congratulations," Judie said to Marge after her team had broken the game's predetermined end mark, twenty points.

"Thanks," she said, walking to the drinking fountain. "But we both know that you were the only thing going for your team. Are those guys freshmen or what?" she asked, indicating Judie's two younger teammates.

"I guess so," Judie said. "You're good, though, Marge."

"Thanks," she said, "but you *are* better. Before tonight, I didn't think so. I thought you were a fraud. A cocky one at that." The two girls laughed.

"Does the girls' team hate me?" Judie asked.

Marge looked away. "No," she began, then, looking at Judie, she said, "yeah, maybe. But they don't realize how good you are." She smiled. "Judie, I'm not saying you're too good for us because you're not. I'm just saying you've got a right to play with the boys. You're better than some of them, and you've got a right to be there. Personally, I was worried that you might make a laughing stock of yourself, and I hated you for that possibility more than anything else. What we don't need is for more people to laugh at girl ball players. They laugh enough already."

Marge got up to get another drink. Judie followed. "Did you ever think about trying out for the boys' team?" she asked Marge.

"Sure," Marge said, "I daydreamed about it. But I'm not good enough. Oh, maybe I could beat out some of the sophomore guards this year. But on the girls' team, I can play with the best of them. That's more my

32

style. . . . It was nice playing with you, Judie. I've gotta go now. See you."

When Marge left, Judie went into the lobby to find Tack, and saw Russ and Boyd playing Ping-Pong. Judie tried to get enough nerve to go in and talk to them, but just as she started toward them, Amy Denniston walked up and started talking to Russ. Amy was a perfect cheerleader; her violet eyes, dark features, and perfect ivory complexion reminded Judie of Liz Taylor in *National Velvet*. Judie had thought for some time that Amy was interested in Boyd. But now, she was talking exclusively to Russ, and when the two of them went over to the soda machine and he bought her a soda, Judie's heart started beating faster. Judie felt the same panic that seized her when the phone rang in the middle of the night: something's wrong.

Tack grabbed her by the shoulder. "What's wrong with you, woman? I got another game set up, so come on." He jogged back into the gym and she followed. She played poorly the rest of the night.

Chapter Six

Judie was sitting in Biology, her first-hour class, when the office assistant came in and gave Ms. Piersall a memo.

"Judie," she said, reading the note, "you're to go to Mr. Vance's office." The young teacher looked at her, then said, "Don't worry about the notes. You can get them later."

Judie picked up her spiral and textbook and left the room. She couldn't figure out why the vice principal wanted to see her. Had someone died in her family? Were her transcripts from Bookner messed up? As she put her books in her locker, she suddenly realized what the trouble was—basketball.

Mrs. Ellis, the secretary, told her to take a seat outside, and that the vice principal would call her when he was ready. As Judie sat there, trying to figure out what Mr. Vance would say and how she would respond, she recognized Coach Arthur's voice coming from inside the office. She strained to understand, but all she could hear was snatches of conversation. "I didn't think it would happen," she heard the coach say, "but it did. When I realized that my plan for her to be an inferior ball player failed—and that she was worth keeping—that's when I changed my mind." Judie couldn't hear what was said next because they began talking in more hushed tones, and it worried her.

Judie had just picked up a magazine when Coach Arthur threw open the door and charged out of the office.

"Come in, Judie," Mr. Vance said from the doorway.

Judie entered his office and sat in the chair opposite his desk. She was nervous, and she knew he knew it.

"Tell me, Judie," he said, "do you like it here at Meier?"

"Yes, I do," she replied, knowing the niceties were only a soft beginning for a not-so-soft discussion.

"Do you like your classes? Everything going okay?" he probed.

"Sure. Fine," she said. Why was Mr. Vance suddenly interested in her well-being? He hadn't even acknowledged the fact that she was alive before.

"You really wouldn't want to see our school get into any difficulties, would you, Judie?"

He's moving in for the kill, Judie thought. "What do you mean by difficulties, sir?" she asked calculatedly. Make it tough on him, too.

"Come on, Judie, we both know what I'm talking about. Why don't you just play on the girls' team and everyone will be happy. I'm sure Mrs. Forster could use you. I hear you're really a fine player, for a girl," he said, still smiling the same irritating smile.

"I am good," she heard herself say, *"and I like the team I'm on."*

He clasped his hands together and wheeled his chair around so he could look out the window as he spoke. "Judie, Coach Arthur was just in here telling me that he didn't even want you to try out. But instead of causing a big stink—and it would be a stink with women's lib and all—he decided to give you a break." He wheeled back around to look at Judie. As he started to speak, he leaned toward her as though he were going

35

to tell her a secret. "The fact is, Judie, you aren't good enough to play on the boys' team. Sure, you'd do fine, maybe even great on the girls' team, but not on the boys'. The boys themselves don't like it either. No one likes it but you, Judie. Don't you think you're being selfish?"

"I don't know," Judie said, shaken. She'd never been in trouble of any magnitude before. She didn't mean to cause trouble.

"Well, it's settled then? You'll quit the boys' team and become our star on the girls' team. I'm sure we'll all be much happier." He stood up, practically lifted Judie out of her seat, and pushed her toward the door.

Judie finally turned to Mr. Vance and spoke. "No," she said emphatically. "I'm not quitting." And then she turned to walk away.

"We're not through," Mr. Vance said through gritted teeth. "And don't you think we are, Miss Conklin."

That day at lunch, Judie told Tack the whole story. He got mad, too, and they sat there the entire period talking about what a poor administrator and terrible human being Vance was. When the first bell rang, she and Tack walked back to her locker, and Cassie was there getting her books, too.

"Hello, stranger," she said to Judie sarcastically.

Judie felt badly. She hadn't done anything with either Cassie or Ann since basketball practice got started. She and Tack were together constantly, and she hardly ever thought about doing anything with anybody but him. "I'm sorry, Cassie," she said, not knowing what else to say.

"It's okay," she said, "I understand you're busy. Give me a call pretty soon, though, okay? Let me know how things are." Cassie pushed her glasses up nervously, and glanced away.

"Sure," Judie said, waving a good-bye to Tack who was leaving for his fifth-hour class. "I've been meaning to call you, Cassie, but the team keeps me so busy."

"I understand, really," she said, "but I haven't even had a chance to tell you the news—I have a date with Chip Baker this weekend." She hugged her books and rolled her eyes. Judie thought she was overdoing it, especially for Chip Baker, but she feigned a smile and said, "Congratulations."

"I know that I must seem pretty second-rate these days," Cassie said, "what with Tack and everything. He's really cute. And you tried to tell me you two weren't dating."

"We're not," Judie said softly, stunned that Cassie refused to understand.

"Sure, Judie," Cassie said, tapping Judie on the shoulder. "I'll bet Lisa Lenney could scratch your eyes out. Tack took her out that one time in late September, then you step in and it's all over. Must be tough, though, with all the razzing you get from the other guys."

"They don't razz me that much," Judie said, "except for Franky and Steve. They love to razz me. But you're wrong about Tack and me. Honest." The bell rang.

"I've got to run," Cassie said, "but we can talk later."

"Okay, Cassie, see you later," Judie said as she turned to go to class. She met Mr. Vance in the hall, but he pretended he didn't see her.

"Good afternoon, Mr. Vance," she said loudly to his back, but he didn't answer. It didn't matter, though, because she knew he'd heard her.

Chapter Seven

"Want to play a game of Horse?" Tack asked, holding the basketball.

"Sure, why not?" Judie said. "It can't hurt my free-throw percentage any." Here, in Judie's back yard, she had little trouble making the free throws that bothered her so much on the court.

Tack put up a shot from fifteen feet out, and it was good. Judie followed suit. When she was sure her shot was good, she said, "You know, Tack, what I said the other night, about sex, I mean, was kind of a lie. I think about it a lot, too." She grabbed the rebound, anxious to have something to do so she wouldn't have to look at him.

"I'm glad," he said. "Maybe we can talk some, if you want to." She passed the ball back to him to set up another shot.

They were both silent for a little while, then finally, as he missed his first shot, Tack said, "Have you ever thought you were in love?"

"No," Judie answered. "Except for the basic junior high crush on a teen idol sort of thing." She smiled. "I was crazy for Donny Osmond of all people. All my friends were gaga over Shaun Cassidy, but not me."

"I guess you must go for teeth," he said, laughing. "But I have to admit that my idol was none other than Laurie on *The Partridge Family* television show." They both laughed freely and ribbed each other. Tack started humming "Puppy Love" and a few other Osmond tunes, so Judie countered with "I Think I Love You."

Judie took the ball and made another shot, then stopped. "Have you ever had sex, Tack?"

"Not really," he said.

"Either you have or you haven't."

Tack was obviously embarrassed. "You don't have to tell me, Tack," Judie said, sorry that she'd put him on the spot.

"No," he said, "I'd like to talk to you, but it's embarrassing. If what I had was sex, then I think I got cheated." His mood lightened up a little, and he started sounding like the old Tack. "It's a torrid romance between a fifteen-year-old boy and his neighbor, a nineteen-year-old college woman who missed the hell out of her boyfriend. Really, it wasn't like I had too much to do with anything. It's not even like I was there, practically. In fact, though I've never said this before, it makes me cringe to think about it."

"Are you trying to tell me you felt 'used'? I thought that's what the woman is supposed to feel after an encounter like that."

He took the basketball and put it on the ground, then rested his foot on it. "I know it sounds funny, but it's the truth. I know that young guys are supposed to be incredibly lucky to have a mature woman teach them, but..."

"I'd hardly label nineteen-year-old women 'mature' across the board, Tack," she said, walking over to where he was standing. She reached down and picked up the basketball.

"Anyway," Tack said, grimacing at Judie for interrupting him, "I'm just saying that I don't think of it as my 'first time.'" He sat down on the cold ground and crossed his long legs. "I'm saving myself, my first time, for something more."

"Let me get this right. You're saving yourself?"

"Not for marriage, dopey. Just for something better than what I had before."

"Well, I can understand wanting it to be more than just casual sex, but to say you're not going to call it your 'first time' is weird. That phrase is given too much emphasis if you ask me. It scares people. It's like either you're a virgin or you're not."

"But that's right. Either you are or you aren't."

"There's a lot in between. And it seems dumb to say that because you've either had sex or you haven't that you deserve a label like virgin. What's the opposite of 'virgin' for a guy?"

"Stud? Something like that?"

"Right. What's the opposite of 'virgin' for a girl?"

"I don't know. But there's not the same kind of stigma that there used to be," he said. "And we're getting off-track. I wanted more of a relationship with sex than I had before. I didn't like to think of it as my 'first time' solely on the grounds that it didn't really feel like I was there. So it doesn't count."

Judie thought about what Tack said. It was like the fact that her name was spelled different from most Judys, and she hated it when people said that she spelled it wrong. Her name was her name, and she should be able to spell it any way she felt like it. She explained her analogy to Tack. "I know it's weak," she said, "but it's sort of the same thing. You could call your fifty-sixth time your first time if it felt like the first time you've actually done it."

"Good woman," he said. "I knew you'd understand. Now, how about you? Are you a 'stud' like good old Tack?" he asked, mocking himself.

"Afraid not," Judie said, "but not for any traditional reasons. In fact, it makes me kind of mad when I think about how it would please some of my family if they knew. Make them think they'd raised me 'right' and all that crap. Fact of the matter is I just haven't found Mr. Right yet."

Tack nodded his head. "But it doesn't keep you from thinking about it, huh?" he asked teasingly. "And that's what makes it so damned important. Even if you don't want to do something dumb or risky, you can't always get it off your mind."

"What are your fantasies like, Tack?" she asked, feeling very comfortable now with him and the subject.

"Oh," he said, beginning to laugh a little timidly, "to be quite honest, they're mostly vague. Parts of bodies smashing together pleasantly, if that's possible. The situations may be different, but the end usually turns out the same."

"Who are they about?"

"Hold on, this isn't fair," he complained, but his objections were short-lived. "Do you really want to know?"

"Sure."

"Will you tell if I tell?"

"Maybe. But not necessarily."

"Okay." He leaned over close to her and whispered as if there were spies just waiting to hear. "Ms. Piersall."

"The biology teacher?"

"Shhh," he said, putting his index finger to his lips, "do you want your mom to know you hang around a guy who has fantasies about a woman who dissects frogs for a living?"

She laughed, then said, "Yours has some distance.

Mine is too close, so I think I'll exercise my option not to tell you." She crossed her arms, and pushed her long blond hair behind her shoulders dramatically.

"I know you've got the hots for Russ Dwyer," he said, "and I think it's great."

Judie was shocked, and her face confirmed the accuracy of his guess. "How did you know?" she asked, worried that others might have noticed, too.

"Relax. Friends can just tell. You should've told me. Are your fantasies kind of crazy like mine?"

"Definitely," she said, beginning to grin again. "Tack, do you realize people think we're dating?"

"I get it all the time from the guys."

Judie thought about telling him about how Lisa Lenney wanted to scratch her eyes out, but he stopped her before she could.

"I wouldn't want to date you, Judie," Tack said, "I couldn't stand to lose my best friend."

Just then, as the night was setting in, Judie noticed the moonlight on his hair, and she thought Tack was the most beautiful and precious person in the world. His hair seemed blonder and his eyes sparkled under the light, and his determined jaw and straight nose were perfect. Judie thought wildly that he was *really* too good to be true. They hugged for a moment, then he picked up the basketball and headed home.

Chapter Eight

Judie was fighting Marty Brondel for a rebound when Franky entered the gym. She didn't turn to look at him, though, until some of the guys started wolf-whistling. There stood Franky, hands on hips, with a pair of footballs stuffed under his T-shirt. "Throw me the ball, you guys," he lisped mockingly. "You guys know I can play with the best of you, if you know what I mean."

No one knew just what to make of him, Judie included, but everyone laughed. About that time, Franky made his way over to Judie, tickling different guys and saying "Hey there, big fella" as he passed them. When he got to Judie, he stood by her side, surveyed her body from top to bottom, and said, "I believe mine are bigger than yours," as he put his hands under his footballs.

The laughter echoed off the high ceiling. Though embarrassed, Judie laughed, too. It's all in fun, she thought to herself, even though she sensed that some of the guys were laughing *at* her as much as at his joke. She grabbed a basketball rolling past her, and she set up a shot, hoping to cut the hilarity short. It didn't work. After dribbling toward the basket, she noticed the laughter was picking up again. When she turned to see, Franky cut short an obscene gesture, and the guys laughed more.

Franky strutted over to Judie once more, encouraged by the support of his little audience. He put his arm around her shoulders and said, "Is it as hard for you as it is for me when you're having your—you know." He paused for effect and finished in a loud whisper, "Your monthlies?"

Amid the howls of laughter, Russ spoke out. "That's not funny, Franky," and he threw the basketball he'd been holding at him and knocked out his football chest. More laughter.

Never to be outdone, Franky picked up the footballs and shoved them back under his shirt. "That's no way to cop a look at a girl's chest, Mr. Dwyer," Franky said, strutting across the gym floor in mock disgust, primping each step of the way.

Again, he stopped and tickled several of the players, calling them "Tiger" and "Big guy" and "Handsome." He circled back and stopped next to Judie, all eyes on him.

She looked at him without any semblance of a smile. Her dad would've told her that if she'd laugh along with them, they'd leave her alone. But even her father wouldn't believe this.

This time, Franky had gone too far. She'd been humiliated more than once during this episode, and she wasn't going to take any more. Despite her strong "time for action" feelings, Judie wished Franky would just let it drop so she wouldn't have to do anything. Wouldn't have to prove herself again. She waited for Franky to strike first.

He faced her squarely this time and dropped the lisp when he spoke. "Isn't this fun, Judie? Aren't you glad you decided to play on the boys' team?" He turned to his audience and smiled during the silence, then swung back to Judie and said, "Maybe you'd like to spend a little time with each of us, just to get to know us better.

Several of us would like to get to know you better." He put his hand on her shoulder.

He wasn't done, that was for certain. Like always, Franky's jokes got bigger and bigger, and Judie knew he was setting her up for some magnificent joke. But while Franky was getting ready for his grand finale, Judie looked at the group watching. Franky's insults were being met with mixed reviews. As they got progressively worse, some of the guys laughing loudly earlier were now only smiling. Some were frowning. Some had walked away in disgust. But the few who had remained, still laughing, took Judie by surprise. They were guys she'd thought of as good people, friends even. Their eyes were filled with contempt.

Franky finished. "Like I was saying, Judie. Spend a little time with each of us. It isn't fair that Tack gets all the action. Spread yourself around a little, if you get my drift."

Guys who had walked away earlier turned back to see Judie's reaction. Tack's anger was apparent, and Judie knew he wanted desperately to strike out, but she looked at him and shook her head. The rest of the group was still. As she glanced around the gym, she felt tears come to her eyes. In the silence, Judie felt that even Franky was beginning to feel badly that he had taken it so far. He squirmed, then as he started to walk away and let it be, Judie stopped him. "Franky," she said in a clear, even voice. He turned, and Judie let the tension build a little before she said, "You're such a *little* prick."

She let herself breathe again, and she could tell the audience had been satisfied, but they were still quiet and unmoving. As she passed Franky en route to the locker room, she noticed the figure of Coach Arthur standing cross-armed in the doorway. He smiled.

"The party's over, Mr. Warnik. Go get ready to play basketball." The coach walked to the center of the gym. Franky didn't move. The coach stopped next to Franky and stood facing him, still cross-armed, without speaking.

"Coach," Franky started, "it was all a joke. Just having a little fun, you know." The coach never moved, and he stared hard at the fidgety boy. Franky tried again in his rambling fashion to make peace with the man. After a few tries without any response from the coach, Franky just stared back trying to gage his anger. Finally, Franky asked, "Do you want me to go change?"

"What did I say earlier, Franky?" the coach said sarcastically in quiet tones. Some of the guys began to laugh quietly, and as Franky walked past Judie, she didn't even smile triumphantly; she just stared.

Tack walked over to Judie once they started practicing and said, "You did a good job."

Judie turned to him, her blue eyes flashing angrily. "Well, where the hell were you?" she asked, nonsensically, knowing he had wanted to help but that she hadn't let him.

Tack grabbed her arm. "Look, Judie, don't shut me out. I'm sorry it happened, but you've got to shake it off. If I could've done something, you know I would have."

"I know, Tack," Judie said apologetically. "I appreciate you. I really do. But today, it just was different out there. I don't know how to explain it." She shrugged, then started to jog toward a stray basketball, but Tack followed.

He looked at her with the look that meant he wasn't leaving without an answer. Judie knew that look. "Okay," she said. "It's just that I don't understand why he hates me. Why any of those guys hate me."

Tack started to say that nobody hated her, but Judie cut him off. "Don't lie to me, Tack. We both saw the way they looked at me." Instead of trying to answer her, something he couldn't have done, he put his arm around her shoulder and gave her a quick hug.

Coach Arthur yelled "Cienelli!", but when Tack turned to look at the man, his face softened, and he said, "Never mind, Tack. Nothing."

After the session ended, the Coach passed out uniforms and discussed the first game of the season. Judie stared at the red cloth and the white number and team name—the Mavericks had better looking uniforms than the Bookner Bluejays' blue and gold, but Judie simply didn't feel the same about wearing it.

Chapter Nine

"I can't believe I'm going to be sharing the guard spot with Franky," Judie moaned as she and Tack approached her car in the parking lot. "After all the crap he pulled today and then, wouldn't you know it, the Coach pops off something like that."

"It's a lousy break. But it beats sitting on the bench while Franky and someone else start for the B team," Tack offered.

"Maybe. Okay, you're right, but I just don't think my mind and Franky's mind will ever connect—on court or off." She unlocked her side of the car, got in, then leaned across the seat to unlock the passenger side. She and Tack had been carpooling the last few weeks, and they'd had fun. It had helped Judie's cause when she approached her parents about getting to drive to school; it was cheaper than having her mom drive to the school and pick her up after practice every day.

"Maybe he'll lay off you once the season really starts."

"Don't count on it," Judie said, trying to find a radio station. "I hate afternoons. KAAY never comes in clear this time of day." Once she found an acceptable station, she turned to Tack and slapped his knee. "By the way, I forgot to congratulate you. Tell me, do varsity players make it a habit of bestowing the glory of their presence on lowly B-team players?"

Tack chuckled. "At least today. I expect to get a phone call any day now from the Boston Celtics asking me to drop out of high school to play for them." He blew on his fingertips in mock conceit.

Judie stopped the car in the middle of the parking lot, glanced at Tack, and said, "Does the Prince wish to walk home?" They both laughed, and Tack muttered "smart ass" loud enough for her to hear.

"Should I ask Lisa Lenney out again?" Tack asked when they were stopped at a stop light.

"Do you want to?"

"Well, I think she'd go with me. At least that's what Maggie Combs says. We sit together in Art."

"You don't really sound too thrilled by the idea."

"I don't know, Judie, it's just that I like Lisa, and she's cute and everything, but she's just so giggly and sweet all the time. It makes me want to puke sometimes the way she always smiles. Always. The girl never frowns; I have been paying attention." Judie looked at him quizzically. "You don't believe me, I can tell. It's the truth. If she'd just snarl once or say 'shit' or something, I'd ask her out again." Tack began fiddling with the radio tuner.

"Tack, I think there must be some other reason, too. I mean, if you liked her, you'd ask her out. Not saying 'shit' often enough is not a legitimate excuse. Let's hear it."

"You're a real know-it-all sometimes, woman. Maybe that *is* all of it. At least, it's as much as I can put my finger on. She's *too* sweet."

Judie maneuvered her mom's Buick into Tack's driveway. She left the engine idling as Tack got out. "Don't you want to come in for something to eat?"

"No," Judie answered, "I'd better get home before my mom has a cow. We were late getting out tonight."

"Okay. I'll see you tomorrow morning. I'll be there around a quarter till, okay?"

"That's fine. You can just honk if you want. My folks are broken in to that now."

Tack waved that he'd heard her, but as he opened the front door and as Judie had started to back out of the driveway, he ran to the car and motioned for her to roll down her window.

"What do you think about Sara Fielder?"

"Huh?" Judie asked. Tack could come up with the silliest conversation topics.

"Do you like her?"

"Marge Fielder's little sister?"

"Yeah. She's not that much younger than Marge. She's a sophomore," he said defensively.

"I wasn't being critical. God knows I was a sophomore last year. It's just that that's the only way I know her—through Marge. Anyway, she seems nice. Why?"

"I think I'm in love with her."

"Good grief, Tack, don't you think you're jumping the gun a little? Try 'like' first, okay?"

"You're harping on meaningless terms, Judie. I'm crazy about her. I've talked to her seven times this week. I've thought about her practically all the rest of the time except during basketball and when I'm with you. She even says 'shit.' What more could I ask for?"

"Move over, Ms. Piersall, former object of lust," Judie said, smiling.

"I'll never trust you with my fantasies again, woman." He started walking toward the house again.

Judie stuck her head out the window and yelled, "That's what you get for hanging around low-life B teamers." She revved up the engine and pulled out of the drive. On the way home, she allowed herself to feel good about being named a starting guard for the B team, even though she made fun of it to Tack. Starting guard. Not bad for a girl, she thought crazily. Not bad for Judie Conklin.

She didn't think about Franky or what had happened early in the practice or about her trig quiz or about Amy Denniston. As she drove, she sang along with the disco single that was topping the chart even though she professed a hatred for disco music. Today everything sounded good.

Chapter Ten

While Judie was dressing out in the girls' restroom off the gym lobby, she could hear the crowd entering the gym. A couple of junior high girls came in while Judie was pulling up her socks, and Judie was glad they hadn't entered sooner. The girls obviously couldn't figure out what she was doing there, and the more outspoken one asked her just why she was dressing out.

"The home team uses the boys' gym dressing room and our boys are in the other dressing room. I don't particularily want to dress in front of either group." Judie laughed, and the girls followed suit. They left without even so much as washing their hands; Judie guessed she'd given them something to talk about.

She didn't really care much about having to dress in the public facility; she was too worried about the game. As she sat on the concrete floor, wishing for a bench to sit on, tieing her shoelaces, she started listening to the crowd. How would they react? Most of the Meier fans had long since heard the complaints of their children, but Judie wondered about the opposition. Did they know she'd be playing? She saw Coach Arthur arguing with Mr. Vance in the hallway earlier that day, and Cassie told her after lunch that she'd overheard Mr. Vance tell Mrs. Ellis that he wanted to see Judie in his office before school let out. Judie worried during fifth, sixth, and seventh hours about being called in, but she finally figured that the coach had saved her from the wrath of Mr. Vance. The team acted normal at the pre-game meeting. They hadn't dressed out or practiced, but they talked about game strategy. They got to go home early, and as the coach dismissed them, he called Judie over to discuss the facility problems and the make-do solution.

As Judie reached to put her sweats in her gym bag, three older women walked in. Maybe it was because she was sitting on the floor, Judie tried to rationalize, or perhaps because she looked like a suited-out boy from the lady's perspective; in any case, the shortest woman let out a scream. Judie felt like the Elephant Man's younger sister, and all she could do was run out of the room.

Tack was waiting for her in the lobby, and as she went tearing out of the restroom, he caught her by her arm. "What's wrong?" he asked.

Judie explained through tears, and she couldn't control her fear any longer. "I don't want to play, Tack. I can't do it. They're going to boo me, you know?"

"No," he said trying to console her, "they won't." They walked outside at her insistence, and they went to the front of the building, out of everyone's sight, and sat down on a cement bench.

For several minutes, Judie cried unashamedly and Tack held her. Then he spoke, "If they laugh, Judie, or boo you, it's because they don't know how to react. They'll respect you when they see how well you play. Just this afternoon, Boyd and I talked about how you really should have been named varsity."

"That's just it, Tack. Why should I have to wait until they can see I play decent basketball before they respect me? They won't laugh at Brondel or any of the sophomores, and I'm better than all of them. It's me. Just me!" She got up and paced back and forth in front of Tack. "They all want me to quit."

"What?"

"They'd all like for me to quit so they can think they were right. They could say that I'd bowed to the pressure, that I wasn't cut out for boys' basketball, that I couldn't compete. They'd love to be able to say that. That's why Franky keeps it up, and that's why Mr. Vance treats me so crummy. They want me to quit before they have to face the fact that I'm good enough."

"In a way, you're kind of like Jackie Robinson, you know, the first black baseball player allowed in the majors. The people gave him all that shit because they didn't want him in their all-white league. Nobody ever thought he wasn't good enough."

"Well," Judie said, calming down as she sat by Tack, "I wonder how far the analogy goes. Do you think that having a girls' team and a boys' team is like segregation? Like 'Separate but Equal'? It kind of makes sense—just look at the money allocated to the boys' team as compared to that of the girls' team. They say that the boys' team draws in more revenue, and supposedly that's why they get more money spent on them, but how much does that have to do with what's right? The Negro Leagues had players just as good as their white counterparts, and yet they didn't draw in the crowds or the money like the majors. And certainly now that there's no racial divisions, blacks have proven they're just as good."

"Whoa, Socrates," Tack said, holding his hands up like a policeman holding up traffic. "You'd better get in there and warm up. It's after six."

Judie started jogging toward the gym, leaving Tack behind. She heard him yell, "I'll be rooting for you!" as she walked through the propped-open door of the gym.

She waved an acknowledgment, and started psyching herself up.

The team was warming up, and she could see that the coach had begun to worry about her whereabouts. She waved at him before grabbing a basketball, and Russ soon came over to her and said, "I'm glad you made it." He smiled. "We're going to need all the help we can get."

The buzzer sounded after what seemed like only seconds to Judie, and the team ran to the sidelines for last minute instructions. The referee signaled for the game to begin, and again the buzzer sounded. The loudspeaker blasted out the five names of the opposition who were starting the game. As she heard the name "Judie Conklin" called out, Judie ran on court amid cries of support and gales of laughter and boos. She barely heard any of it, though, because her own heart was ringing loudly in her ears. When the starting Meier five met on court, they huddled momentarily and shouted, "Let's go!" before assuming their positions.

Meier got the tip and scored first. Judie's opponent was an inch shorter than she, and was less adept at ball handling. Franky's guard, on the other hand, was very good, and Franky had trouble keeping up, even early in the first quarter.

Soon, Judie noticed that Franky never threw her the ball. When she got it, it was from one of the forwards or from Pete Dalton, the center. It was no longer an oversight or a coincidence, Judie decided, and she wondered how long it would take the coach to realize it. While bringing the ball down court, the little guard slapped her hand while trying to take the ball away from her.

"One and one," the referee called out, indicating Judie had free throws coming to her.

She panicked. "They don't have five team fouls yet, sir," she told the referee. "Don't we just take the ball out?"

"You're right, young lady." He took the ball to the sidelines and handed it to Franky. Franky slapped the ball and tried to find an open player.

Judie lost her guard and was free under the basket. She motioned wildly, but Franky ignored her. He threw it to Pete, who was far less open than Judie, but Pete soon saw Judie and fed it to her for the basket.

Coach Arthur called a time-out, and as Judie was running off court, she could see the anger in his eyes. "Why the hell didn't you throw the ball to Judie?" he yelled in a coach's whisper to Franky.

"I didn't see her," he lied.

"Yeah? Well, you haven't been seeing too well the entire game, so why don't you sit down for a while and try to find a little vision somewhere?" The coach turned to look at the bench. "Mike, go in for him."

The whistle sounded, and as Judie was running back on court, the coach grabbed her arm. "Don't shy away from free throws if they want to give them to you. You'll do fine."

"Okay, Coach," Judie said. She ran back to position, and during the remainder of the half, she watched Mike let the guard take over. The Meier lead soon diminished, and Judie soon saw the coach's signal for her to switch opponents with Mike. Mike fared better with the little guard, but Judie knew her new opponent was much more challenging.

She noticed the boy's dribbling was flamboyant, messy, and she soon saw opportunity to try to steal, and even though the coach hadn't called for a full court press, she stayed with him as he brought the ball down.

She knocked it away from him, but they both scrambled for the loose ball.

"Jump!" cried the referee.

As the two sets of players got into position, the taller guard said, "Lay off me, bitch," as they prepared to jump. Judie once again noticed the noisy crowd, something she'd barely given heed to since the beginning of the game, and the butterflies returned. Franky could out jump this guy, she told herself, if only I were taller...

The ball was tossed, and Judie sensed that the over-confident boy had jumped too soon; his timing was off. As Judie sprang up for the toss, she knew it was hers. The appreciative roar of the crowd was of little consequence as she watched her teammates march the ball downcourt for the score.

Chapter Eleven

As Judie pushed open the doors at McDonald's, she looked around for a booth where both she and Tack could sit. Tack followed, his blond hair still slightly wet from the showers, and he was flying high. Not only did the varsity win, but Tack played a full quarter and then some. Judie was disappointed that the B team had lost, but she was happy with the way she'd played.

While they searched the room for a spot, Judie looked at all the girls from school and how they were dressed. She was wearing her usual tan sweater and corduroys, and she wondered if the other kids worried about the way they looked as much as she did lately. She didn't want to change her style, but she found herself thinking more often about her appearance. Tonight it was important that she fit into off-court action as well.

"There's one," Tack said, indicating a booth in the rear of the store next to where some of the team was gathering. Judie glanced at Tack—the blue sweater he was wearing looked terrific on him—then followed him to the table.

"Here comes Julius Irving Cienelli and Magic Johnson Conklin," yelled Anthony Northe, the varsity center. "You both played great."

They both muttered a "Gee, thanks," sat down in the next booth, and got in on the conversation.

"That was a great play, Tack, you know, the one

where you slapped that guard's hand while he was shooting. Remember? The guy who made *both* free throws?" jibed Northe.

"Give me a break, will you? There happened to be a great big brown recluse spider crawling on his wrist. Thought maybe I'd forfeit two lousy points for a human life, you know? Boy, but you guys are inhuman," Tack said, shaking his head in disbelief.

Everyone laughed, saying "Sure, Cienelli" or "Yeah, don't give me that" or "What a brave soul!" Judie wished for a moment that she had Tack's timing and wit—or either one.

When some of the post-game excitement had simmered down, Judie poked Tack and pointed across the room to where Sara Fielder was sitting. He turned red, then pretended he was too busy talking to say anything to her.

"You're a chicken, Tack. Go over there and just talk to her about the game. She won't bite," Judie teased.

"I know," he said, "but the fact is that I don't want to be rejected. Rumor had it that she's got a date tomorrow night with some dumb football player."

"That's funny. I've never heard anything about it. And Marge didn't mention it this afternoon when we discussed the two of you."

Tack's mouth literally dropped open. "Judie, you didn't. You didn't, did you? Come on, say you didn't."

"I think I'll get a Coke," she said, standing up.

"No way," Tack said, pulling her back down. "Let's hear it."

Judie couldn't help smiling. "What's to hear? Marge said something about Sara not wanting to play basketball even when they were little, and I said my big brother always forced me to play. Then she said that Sara had learned to like to watch, and I said that she

59

probably couldn't help liking it after being around Marge so much. Then she said that Sara was around all her friends a lot, and as a result, Sara goes to all the games to see the girls play. And she said that Sara usually goes to the boys' games, too, and I said that you thought she—Sara, I mean—was really neat, and Marge said that Sara had mentioned that she liked you, too." Judie put her hands behind her head as if she were bored with the topic.

"What else did she say?"

"Let me think," Judie said, pondering. "Oh, yeah, she said that she thought the girls' team would do well this year because they have a better center...."

"Not about the team, Judie, about Sara. What else did she say about Sara?"

"Nothing," Judie answered, then looked away. Before Tack had time to grill her, Russ and Boyd walked up to the booth. Boyd sat down in the last spot in the booth next to theirs.

"Got room for me?" Russ asked.

"Sure we do," Judie said, getting ready to scoot over when Tack moved and Russ scooted in next to him. The three of them listened to the general discussion about the game at the next booth, interjecting things sometimes, but always as part of the main conversation and never just to each other. Once, when Russ had turned to answer a question, Tack winked at Judie, pointing to Russ, and gave her the okay sign with his hand. Judie glared at him, but he just shook his head, saying she deserved it.

"That guard you finally had to take wasn't too shabby, huh, Judie?" Mike Dale asked. "He ran circles around me."

"Gary Coleman could run circles around you, Dale," Tack said, and everyone laughed.

"Shut up, Tack," Judie said, "or I'll bring up the spider again." Tack smiled, then put up his hands, surrendering.

"That was great when you out jumped that guy," Russ said to Judie, "and I really didn't think you could do it. You know, I..."

"Where'd Boyd go?" Tack asked Russ, interrupting him.

"Over there," Russ said, pointing to a group of Pep Club girls sitting with Sara Fielder.

"He's just making time, I see," Tack said. "I just hope he doesn't try to make time with Sara," he said under his breath to Judie.

"What?" Russ asked.

"Nothing," Tack replied. "I think I'll go see how Boyd's doing. He played a terrific game." Tack winked at Judie, then Russ got out of the booth to let Tack out. He slid back in to the middle of the booth so he was sitting directly opposite Judie.

"Well," Russ said, "you played really well tonight. I bet it was kind of rough walking out there in front of the crowd and everything."

"Yes," Judie said, "it was." She wished she had a Coke or some tea so she would have something to do with her hands while they spoke.

The silence was getting thick. "You played well, too, Russ," Judie said. "You're so much better than Brondel."

"Thanks," he said. "Brondel's got a lot to learn about defense."

They both pretended to listen to the basketball play-by-play that the next table was reenacting, but both tried to think of things to say to each other.

"Have you seen that new Streisand movie?" Russ asked.

"No, I haven't," Judie answered.

"I heard it's really funny. It's playing here in town."

"Really? I read a review that said it was really crummy but you know how reviewers love to give Streisand movies bad reviews."

"Yeah," he said. "Listen, if you're not doing anything..."

A body appeared at the table, and both Judie and Russ glanced up to see who it was.

"Hi, Russell," Amy Denniston said.

"Hi, Amy," Russ said, red-faced. "Uh, Amy, do you know Judie? Judie Conklin, I'd like you to meet Amy Denniston."

"Hi," Judie said, hiding disappointment.

Amy smiled, then said to Russ, "Listen, Russ, the gang I'm with is going over to campus. There's a dance there, and Boyd said to tell you that he's got some beer. He's waiting in the car."

She stood there patiently, without asking for an answer. Judie thought she was really nervy, standing there as if she knew he'd want to go with her. But Boyd was going, Judie knew, and that meant Russ would likely follow. If only he'd finish his question about the movies, Judie thought.

"Well," he said finally, glancing up first at Amy, then back at Judie, "I guess I'd better go. Boyd's my ride, after all." He got up and slid out of the booth, and as Amy started to walk off, he turned to Judie and said, "See you later, Judie."

"Yeah," Judie said, "later."

Judie wondered if she should have asked him to the movies. She thought of herself as a feminist, basically, though she wished she knew more about feminism. One day, she told herself, she would read all the literature good feminists read, but right now, she was satisfied knowing the basics and acting on her feelings. She knew that asking Russ out was her right, but she also knew it would be awkward at best. Having the right didn't always make it feel good. Maybe she should've insisted somehow on going with the group to campus. But that wasn't her style, either. What was her style? Whatever it was, she decided, it wasn't working.

Sitting there with nothing but Russ's empty soda cup, Judie wondered whether her basketball career had anything to do with her deplorable social life. Not that Tack wasn't the best friend she'd ever had, but she had feelings that Tack didn't satisfy which couldn't be ignored any longer. It was all so damned hard. Judie hated playing the games that went with dating. If only she could act natural around Russ, the way she acted when she was with Tack, everything would be great. The one time she had some confidence built, and was certain Russ was at least interested in her, Amy Denniston just busted her way into Judie's life and destroyed everything. What bothered her the most, she decided, was that she couldn't control what happened to her—that someone else controlled her feelings. Was this what love was all about?

On the way home, Judie and Tack were silent. He hadn't done so well with Sara, he said as he started the car. She didn't mention the Amy incident, and she didn't want to talk about her feelings. Tack was wrapped up in his own, and for once, Judie didn't understand her own feelings well enough to discuss them with anyone. But somehow it felt good just *being* with Tack.

Chapter Twelve

"I did it, Judie," Tack screamed over the phone.

Judie pulled the phone receiver away from her ear. "Not so loud," she said. "Now what did you say?"

"I did it," he said again. "I got a date with Sara Fielder. For tonight."

Judie felt oddly unhappy, but said, "Great, Tack. How'd it happen?"

Tack told her he had gone to the grocery store for his mother and saw Sara in the frozen food section. "So, I went over, then we talked for a while, then I asked her what she was doing tonight. Bingo."

Judie and Tack had made plans the night before to go see the new Streisand movie tonight. Now what would she do? She might see what Cassie or Ann had planned, but she knew she wouldn't have as much fun as she would with Tack. Tack's voice interrupted her thoughts.

"Aren't you proud of me? The girl of my dreams said she'd go out with me."

"I think it's terrific. I knew she would."

"Is something wrong, Judie?"

"No, crazy. I'm just in a funny mood, that's all." Judie feigned excitement for a few minutes, then made up an excuse to get off the phone. She felt like when she got a bad grade on a paper that she thought she'd done well on—kind of cheated.

As she lay on her bed listening to James Taylor, she felt reflective. She remembered some of the better times in her old hometown. She remembered that certain feeling that made her feel good even when things were bad. What was that feeling? She tried to pin it down, but all she could deduce was that it had something to do with her hometown and with being, well, kind of a child. It was a pick-you-up-and-dust-you-off kind of feeling that went with living in Bookner.

That feeling was gone. It wasn't just moving away that stripped her of the feeling—she'd begun to lose it when they were still living there. It felt as though she grew more restless and less protected as time went by. Wasn't becoming an adult supposed to make you feel more mature? Or at least more able to take care of yourself? Judie wasn't sure, but she did know that growing up didn't always feel good. One day life was exciting and challenging, the next day life was overwhelming.

When "Don't Let Me Be Lonely Tonight" began, Judie began to cry. It made her feel worse just knowing she really didn't have any reason to cry. Her best friend had a date with the girl of his dreams, and here she was, Judie Conklin, aged sixteen, crying over not having anything to do that night. And every second that she felt guilty for not being happy for Tack, she couldn't help thinking that if he and Sara got along, then she'd see less and less of him.

Think about basketball, Judie told herself. Better yet, go practice. Meier had two games this week. She decided to try to get together a pick-up game. Whom should she call? Tack always did the calling and the organizing. She could feel her momentary burst of positive thinking begin to crash. "Don't let it happen," she told herself. "Do it yourself."

She walked into the kitchen to use the phone, but just as she did, her mother walked in from the utility room. "Who are you calling, dear?" her mother asked.

"Just some guys to play basketball," Judie answered, thumbing through the phone book.

"You are not going to call any boys, Judie. I'm putting my foot down," her mother said matter-of-factly.

"Mom," Judie cried out, "that's ridiculous. I'm calling." She kept on thumbing through the phone book. Dwyer, no Russ. What was his father's name? Robert? It sounded right, but the street didn't sound familiar. Tack would know, but if she called Tack, he'd want to play So? she asked herself. Why shouldn't he play?

Her mother grabbed the phone book from her hands. "You do not disobey me, young lady," she said, laying the phone book down on the counter next to the stove. "I think we had better talk about this. You spend all your time lately with that boy, but you say you aren't dating. Then what are you doing all the time? And what about girlfriends? Don't you have any? Judie, your father and I..."

Judie walked out of the room. "Judie, you get back in here. Don't you walk out on me. You are the most belligerent child I have ever seen in my life!" Judie could hear her mother from her bedroom even though she shut the door as she entered. She tried to block out her mother's voice, but without luck. She put on a record and plugged in her headphones. Cris Williamson sang lightly into her head, and she tried not to think about anything besides the music. Everything else hurt.

But Cris's voice was cut off with a swing of her mother's arm. Judie opened her eyes to her mother's figure, standing at the foot of her bed.

"Judie," she said softly, but with a tinge of anger,

"you do not, I repeat, do not leave the room when I am talking to you, understood?"

Judie remained silent.

"I said do you understand?"

Judie looked hard at her mother, and said, "I understand that you don't want to talk *to* me. You want to talk *at* me."

"I not going to argue semantics with you, Judie. All I want you to understand is that you are never again to walk out of the room when I'm talking to you." She paused for effect, then said, "Do you understand me?"

"I understand perfectly," Judie said. When her mother started to leave, Judie said, "Mom, why can't I call the other players to round up a game?"

Her mother looked confused. "Judie, I want you to be normal, do normal things. I don't think it's good for you to hang around basketball players all the time. You need to go to parties—be with girls your own age—have dates. It's time you started acting like..." Her mother looked out the window trying to find the right word.

"Like a girl?" Judie asked sarcastically. "And how do they act?"

"Judie, you may not understand right now, but you will. It doesn't look right the way you hang around boys all the time."

"I don't care how it looks and I doubt that I ever will. How things look to other people is their business and it doesn't have anything to do with the way things really are. Mom, those basketball players you're talking about are my friends. They're terrific, most of them. It's just the most important part of my life right now. You remember when Matt was playing ball. It was all he could think about, too."

"But, Judie, that's what bothers me. It shouldn't be

67

the most important part of your life. You're a sixteen-year-old *girl*."

"What does that have to do with anything? Matt was sixteen, too. The only difference is that he's a boy."

Her mother straightened the books on Judie's desk as she thought of what to say next. "Judie, all I know is that it just isn't right. I don't know how to explain it, but it isn't right."

"Then I don't want to be right," Judie said, turning over onto her stomach. She knew that turning over like that in the middle of the conversation was immature. Once she turned back over, to face her mother though, she was gone.

Judie plugged in the headphones, sat back down on her bed, and cried softly so her mother couldn't hear. She'd been crying too often the last couple of days. It bothered her to cry—it made her feel like a baby. She tried to analyze her mother's point of view; she knew it was the most logical and mature way to look at the argument. But her mother's notions of what a sixteen-year-old girl should be were governed by conventions that Judie didn't believe in. It bothered her mother that she really didn't care what other people thought. Knowing her mother though, she felt a little sorry for her. It was hard disagreeing with and standing up to the person who loves you most in the world, Judie thought. At the same time, Judie promised herself to be on the lookout for more of the "Let's-Turn-Judie-Normal" campaign.

She turned the pages of the season in her mind. She knew if she thought about basketball, she could lose herself in it. Her high game so far was 29 points—third game of the season against Lanoue. Worst game—11 points—fifth game of the season against Richard High School. But those were last year's stats, and in the next

68

few weeks, she'd be playing more games than she'd ever played during her whole life. Homecoming at Meier was in less than a month, and she was sure that the coach would have her playing opposite that Roberts kid from Coleman High who was supposed to be so terrific. She reached over to her desk and looked at the schedule. Van Hook was supposed to be tough. So was Bass. Judie panicked a little when she realized that the next two months were solid Friday night games, and two tournaments during the week. She knew she was the number-one B-team guard, and that she'd have to be the one to oppose the number-one guard of whatever team they played. It made her feel good, but today, she gave way to fear easily.

Judie drifted off into sleep as she thought about floor maneuvers. On the inside of her eyelids rolled the images of her playing. Go left; he's been faked out; Dalton's open; fast-break him; send Franky over to set up the play; back to me; up the center; left-hand lay-up; dribble around him, Marty; set up the zone; come on, you guys, move!

Judie awoke to a knock on her door. "Come in," she said, grabbing a nearby paperback so no one would know she'd been asleep.

Her mother's face appeared through a crack in the door. "Phone, honey," she said softly, "I think it's Tack."

"Tell him I'm in the shower."

Her mother waited silently; Judie knew she meant "no" by her lack of response. She got up and walked into the kitchen, but decided to take it in the family room instead.

"Yeah," she said into the phone. She knew that she had no good reason to be cool to Tack, but she wanted to be nonetheless.

"I'm nervous," he said. "Really nervous."

"Why?"

"What do you mean 'why'? You know why. I'm supposed to pick her up in an hour."

"So pick her up." She didn't like the way she was treating Tack. "It'll be okay, Tack. She's just as nervous as you are."

"I guess so. Hey, the other reason I called is because I want to apologize for messing up our plans without so much as a 'sorry'. It was lousy of me to cancel so late."

"Don't worry about it. I know how it is," Judie said. "Besides, it's no big deal. It'll give me a chance to go out with some other people. I've been meaning to lately anyway."

"Anyway," Tack said, "I'm sorry. Can I treat you to a movie tomorrow afternoon to make up for it?"

Judie started to make up an excuse not to go, but she dismissed the entire "I have plans" routine. "Sure, I think that sounds fair. What do you want to see?"

"You pick. Oh, yeah, I ran into Boyd this morning, too."

"You ran into a lot of people this morning. Are you bruised?"

"Smart ass. He said that I should come down to the Rec Center this afternoon pretty late. They've got a game lined up, but I told him I was busy. He asked me to tell you about it, but I forgot until now. It's only five fifteen. I'd bet you'll still catch them if you want to get some practice in."

"I might. Well, have fun tonight. And relax, okay?"

"Okay. Thanks, Jude. You're a pal," Tack said. "Bye."

"Bye." Judie went back to her room to decide if she wanted to go play. Russ would be there. She needed to practice. She didn't have anything else to do besides feel sorry for herself. She grabbed a sweatshirt, asked to borrow the car, and left within ten minutes. But when she got there, Russ wasn't there.

"Great, Judie," Boyd yelled across the gym floor. "You're just in time. Russ just left to get ready for a date, and shirts need another man."

"You'll have to settle for a woman," Judie yelled back sarcastically, but the guys laughed.

"Sounds good to me," Boyd yelled, tossing her the ball. "Take it out. We're behind 12-8. Russ makes a shitty guard."

She took the ball out of bounds and felt a certain kind of calmness as her palm slapped the worn leather.

Chapter Thirteen

Homecoming Week at Meier began on Monday morning, and as Judie walked with Tack to her locker, she was surprised to see all the decorations on the usually drab walls. Judie looked at Tack as they approached a fake but life-size cougar hanging from the rafters with an attached sign that read: "Kill the Cougars." Tack laughed, then said that Meier always took the homecoming game very seriously.

While she got her books for first hour, Tack told Judie about all the Meier High traditions: hall decorations contests between the classes, spirit contest at the Pep Assembly, the daily dress-up contests, and the Thursday night pre-game parade. "And I thought the extra practices were bad," Judie said with a laugh. They walked to Tack's locker en route to class.

"Have a date with Sara this weekend?" she asked. They had been an "item" at school ever since their date a few weeks before.

Tack nodded. "Well, how'd it go?" Judie asked.

"Okay," he said. He wouldn't look at her.

"What do you mean 'okay'? This was serious girl-of-your-dreams business not long ago. What happened?"

"It was okay, I said. We went to a movie, got some pizza, and watched TV at her house. It was fine."

Judie tried to get a look at his face. "You've got to

give her a chance. Your expectations are a little high, don't you think?"

"Maybe. I guess I expected fireworks."

"Tack, sparklers are fireworks of sorts. They just happen to last longer," Judie said, knowing her philosophy was getting a little sappy. "Just don't expect so much all the time. I hate it when you act so depressed."

He opened his locker and found it covered with glittered streamers, candy bars, notes of encouragement, and a big red heart that was signed "your secret Pep Pal."

"What is all this? From Sara?" Judie asked.

"No, it's another tradition. Pep Pals are members of the Pep Club. Every homecoming game, they each take a player's name and do all kinds of favors for them. It's a secret, obviously," he said, pointing to the heart, "and at the Victory Dance after the game, each of them tells who their player was. It's hokey, but kind of fun."

"Wow, you big varsity guys sure do get all the fun," Judie kidded him.

"B teamers get it, too. I had a Pal last year." Tack noticed Judie's expression, then said, "Maybe your Pal hasn't made it to school yet."

"You kidding? No Pep Clubber wants to be Pals with a girl. What fun would that be? We all know what they're in this for."

"What?" Tack asked.

Judie looked around with exaggerated interest, then said softly, "The sex."

Tack laughed loudly. "Oh boy!" he shouted, shutting his locker door. "That can't be right," he said, "because I sure didn't get any last year."

"That's just because you got one that was a little less peppy," Judie kidded him.

"You are full of it today, aren't you?" Tack asked playfully. They were joking with each other when they passed a massive sign above the junior class bench. "Good luck to all you Meier *BOYS!* (AND WE DO MEAN BOYS)"

"That's real school spirit if you ask me. I wonder if there's a sign anywhere around here that divides the team by religion," Judie said, looking around again.

"Take it easy, Judie, it's not that big a deal."

"Oh, really?" she said, "I want to see one that says 'Good luck to all you Jewish players'? How about 'You white Meier players'? Is there one?" She was jogging up and down the hall a little, looking around wildly, talking loudly.

"Judie," Tack said, taking hold of her arm, "settle down. They're loving it. You're playing into their hands." The kids sitting on the bench began to stare, and it got quiet.

"Can you guys tell me?" Judie said sharply to a group of Pep Club members. "I mean, you painted these signs, right? I'd like to see the 'Down with nigger players' collection. Is it with the anti-communist collection?"

Tack grabbed Judie and tried to pull her away. "Don't let it get to you. They're just immature. It's not worth it."

"Damned if it's not worth it," she said through clenched teeth, pulling away. "Does anyone here claim to have painted that sign?" Judie asked the crowd. "Anyone at all? So no one painted the sign? Well, that's just great."

"I painted it," one girl said. "Me and four other girls. And to tell you the truth, I don't care if you know it or not because everybody is on my side," she said, looking at the few girls standing behind her. They nodded support.

Judie looked at the girl a long time before speaking. "I think it's really lousy of you to judge me like that. To say you've got all this school spirit, but to slap me in the face like that. You don't know me at all. Why do you want to ridicule me through something as dumb as that?"

The girl was silent, as was the rest of the crowd. Several people walking to class stopped to hear Judie. "Have you ever seen me play?" Judie asked.

"No," the girl said, "I only go to varsity games." Her voice was beginning to quiver, and the group behind her started to disperse. The first bell rang.

"Well, I'll tell you what. You come to practice tonight, and if you can honestly tell me that I don't play as well, that I don't belong there, then I'll help you put this sign back up. But right now, it's coming down. Fair enough?"

The girl started nodding her head, and she walked away with her friends.

Tack and a couple of other kids who watched the episode climbed on the bench to take down the sign. "You were great, Judie," Tack said.

"Yeah, what a pig," someone else said.

"I never thought this sign should be up, either." Still another voice.

Judie started walking to class and the second bell sounded. Her second tardy slip of the semester—one more and she'd have to go see Mr. Vance. She silently promised herself that she would not be tardy again.

She heard Tack's voice yell her name down the hall. He ran ahead to catch her. "Don't run," she yelled in a whisper, "we're already late."

When he caught up with her, she could tell something else was wrong. "Russ is down in the principal's office," he said out of breath.

75

"Why?" she asked.

"So's Franky. They got in a fight."

"Over what?" Tack took her arm and motioned for her to follow him. As she approached her locker, she got a sinking feeling that she was the basis of the fight. In big red Magic Marker letters, the word "BITCH" was written lengthwise down her locker door.

"That bastard," she said, starting to cry. Tack again took her arm and maneuvered her to a bench just outside the building—another violation of school rules—but it didn't matter to either of them.

While she tried to stop crying, Tack told the story of the fight. Franky was writing the word on her locker when Russ and Boyd passed. Russ saw that Franky was writing something, and, knowing Franky, stopped to see what it was he was writing. Just as Franky finished, Russ shoved him against the lockers. Boyd got everyone to stand back, including Franky's friends. When a teacher noticed the fight, he tried to break it up, but neither of them would stop. After a few minutes, the teacher came back with two others, and they had to physically restrain the two and take them bodily to the office.

"What should I do?" Judie asked.

"I think we should both go down to the office."

"But you'll be even later to class, Tack. Maybe you should go on."

"Silly woman," Tack said with a grin, "once you're tardy, you're tardy. It won't matter."

They walked back in the building and down to the office. When they got there, Russ was inside with Mr. Vance, and Franky was in Mr. Lord's office. Rarely did Mr. Lord deal with discipline—that was his assistant's job.

As Judie started to explain to the secretary, Mr.

Vance stepped out of his office. "Come in, Judie," he said, "I'm sure you're quite a happy young lady this morning. Just the kind of thing you thrive on, I imagine."

"Now wait a minute," Tack said.

"Who are you?" Mr. Vance asked.

"Tack Cienelli. I'm a friend of..."

"Get to class, Mr. Cienelli. You don't have any business here."

"I think I should stay. I know quite a bit about what has gone on all year long in practice and..."

"I said go to class. Miss Conklin, please come in. Mr. Dwyer was just leaving. Remember, Russ, I'll see you in detention this afternoon."

"But I told you I have basketball practice," Russ said firmly.

"Oh, all right. I'll make it seven thirty just for you. See you tomorrow morning. How's that sound?"

"Peachy."

"That was silly, Russ. One extra morning. Any other smart comments?"

Russ left without another word, and Judie stepped into Mr. Vance's office. He told her about the fight, and Judie knew he was trying somehow to make her feel that she caused the whole thing. "So, it was basically a little practical joke, and Russ couldn't take it," Mr. Vance said.

Judie looked at the man and smiled, then shook her head. "You're something," she said sarcastically.

"Wait a minute now, Judie. Franky was only being a boy—and he'll get his punishment. We wouldn't want the women's libbers to get upset. He'll get three days detention—two for damaging school property and one for fighting. Of course, if he can rub the magic marker off your locker, then he's down to two days of detention."

"So really, he and Russ have the same punishment coming? Is that right? That's absurd."

"Miss Conklin, I don't care what you consider to be absurd; the punishment stands. In fact, though Franky was a bit crude, his writing on your locker was almost a refreshing sort of practical joke—a traditional prank. I like traditions, Judie," he said, smiling a condescending smile.

Judie got up to leave. "Wait, miss," Mr. Vance said, standing. "I'm not through with you. Right before I had to deal with Franky and Russ, there was a young lady down here complaining about *you*. Seems you harassed her in front of her friends about a sign she'd painted."

Judie started to cry out in her defense, but Mr. Vance signaled that he didn't want to hear any excuses. "You're dismissed. But remember, if your behavior continues to be disruptive, I'll see that your punishment is fitting."

"I'm sure you'll see that it's more than fitting, Mr. Vance. Have a wonderful morning." Judie glared at him before shutting the door behind her, but the smile on his face stole what little pleasure she got from the sarcastic remark.

Chapter Fourteen

Judie collapsed in her father's reading chair when she got home from the extra-long practice. The day had taken its toll on her. She felt like a clothesline stretched as far and as tightly as possible. And everyone keeps hanging things on me, Judie reflected.

During practice she could tell that Mr. Vance had discussed her with the coach. Oddly enough, he treated her no differently than other days, except perhaps, that he treated her with a little more respect. Tack once told her that the coach and Mr. Vance were always disagreeing, and after today, Judie believed it.

Her mother came in the room and sat down in the next chair. "How'd things go at school today?" she asked.

"Okay, I guess," Judie said.

Judie could tell from the fact that her mother kept thumbing through a magazine while she spoke that she was up to something.

"Betty Lowery called today."

Judie turned to face her mother. There was more to it than a phone call. "Get to the point, Mom," Judie said defensively.

"Betty's daughter is president of the school Pep Club. Seems they're pretty upset with you."

"How's that?" Judie asked, too tired for another argument.

"According to her, you yelled at one of the members. To hear her tell it, you humiliated the poor girl. Called her names. Made her cry."

"That's not true, Mom. Ask me about it later, okay? I promise to tell you the whole story later, but right now I'm too tired. Okay?" Judie heard her mother get up and go back into the kitchen. Then she listened to whispered snatches of conversation: "Damned team...got no business...acts different these days...just don't know what to do with that girl."

Judie got up and went into her bedroom. Within five minutes she was interrupted by her mother. "Judie, I want you to listen to me. I'm your mother and I think I know what's best for you." Judie knew that what was coming wasn't going to be pleasant—whenever her mother prefaced a discussion with "I'm your mother," Judie knew to expect the worst.

"Are you listening to me?" her mother asked. Judie nodded and continued to brace herself for disaster. "If I hear so much as one more word about your disruptive behavior, you are not going to play ball any more. I simply refuse to let that game ruin our lives."

Judie sensed that her mother was waiting for some sort of outburst, but she couldn't say anything. She felt a little dizzy, but she hid her face in her pillow and tried to hide.

"Do you understand me, Judie?" she asked. "No more disruptions and no more embarrassment."

"Embarrassment? Who's embarrassed?" Judie asked, unable to hide in the comfort of her pillow any longer.

"You'll have to admit, Judie, that your playing on the team causes your father and me embarrassment. Hardly a day goes by that I don't run into someone who doesn't ask about you or say something about your playing on the boys' team. Sometimes they give me hostile looks or they turn their heads. Yes, it is an embarrassment to me." Mrs. Conklin sat down on her daughter's bed, and Judie noticed that her voice was softer; she wasn't talking to Judie, but to herself.

"But Mom, it's not my fault what happened at school today. I didn't start it. Her sign—do you even know what it said? It said that she wished the boys good luck, but not me. It made a point to single me out and *not* wish me luck. I've never done anything to them."

"Judie, you don't have to do anything to them in order for them to dislike you. The fact that you're a good player has nothing to do with it. It all has to do with how you make them feel."

"Well, you're just like them. You've never been to a single game of mine, and you went to all of Matt's. I'm a better player than Matt, Mom. Did you know that? Do you even care?" Judie lashed out with all the energy she had left. She had to feel free to be whatever she wanted, and in order to make that possible, her mother had to understand.

"Listen to me, Judie. I think you'll have a much easier time at school if you would just take the time to understand the other kids' positions."

"Why? They obviously don't care about my position. You've already agreed with me that my point of view and my actions are irrelevant."

"That's true, Judie," her mother said, "and that's why it's so important for you to understand why they don't care. Maybe you'll be able to reach some sort of middle ground, at least with some of them. The ones who are able to see what you are will come to respect you. Those are the only people who really count."

Judie regarded her mother cautiously. Was she trying to help after all?

"Maybe I've been slightly off-track, Judie," she said.

"I have been seeing your playing as something that affected my life and not as something you enjoy. Now, don't get me wrong—I don't approve of all your actions, and you're still going to have to deal with me about this confrontation later. But, I can see your point about having others judge you without trying to see your side. It's the same with the women who give me the hostile stares. They're generally ignorant of how well you play and what kind of kid you are. The ones who've been around you, seen you play, or have kids who like you, are the ones who say something good about you whether or not they agree with what you're doing. I guess you must have it doubly hard because you're in high school—the land of follow-the-leader." Judie's mother walked to the window and peered out, laughing a faraway laugh that Judie knew she was not a part of. It was distant—her mother was distant—and Judie witnessed her mother's flight back into someplace in the past. She stood there a few minutes, and Judie knew not to interrupt, not to make her come back before she had to.

"Rose, have you seen the *Time* magazine?" came the voice from the living room.

Judie wanted to silence her father like her mother used to in order to keep her quiet when her father was asleep, usually one of those times he was working second shift. She felt very protective of her mother at that moment and angry with her father for making her come back. She wished she could talk to her mom like this more often.

But Judie's mother didn't appear disturbed. Her only reaction to her father's voice was an arch of her back, a pull of her shoulders that reminded Judie of pulling on a horse's reins to make him stop. Mrs. Conklin smiled at Judie as she walked out, and Judie felt sad as she heard her mom yell "I think it's on the counter, honey."

Judie put on a record and plugged in her headphones. She thought about what her mom said as she began to relax. Just a few minutes passed when she felt someone shaking her foot to get her attention. Her mom stood at the foot of her bed motioning for Judie to take off her headset. She did.

"Dinner's ready," she said. She stood in the doorway as Judie passed her en route to the dining room, and Judie turned to see why her mother didn't follow. "Judie, do you keep your basketball schedule in your top drawer or your second drawer?"

"Top one, Mom," she said, smiling broadly for the first time all afternoon.

Later that night, when Judie's parents had gone shopping, Judie phoned Russ to apologize for the mess he'd gottin into. She wasn't sure about his father's name, but she tried Robert. A man answered, but it was the wrong number. She looked in the book again. It seemed like he lived in the northeast part, but Judie couldn't find a street that sounded right. Wilson Street? The name listed was Margaret. She tried it. She recognized Russ's voice as soon as he said hello.

"Russ?" Judie asked. "This is Judie. Conklin. I just wanted to call and say how sorry I am about what happened at school today."

"It's not your fault, but I'm sorry it happened, too. Franky refuses to grow up, you know?"

"I know, believe me."

"He makes the team look bad. He acts like he's perpetually twelve years old. He hasn't changed since elementary school."

"You went to elementary school with him?"

"Yeah. I had Boyd and Franky in my first-grade class. I remember Mike Dale and even Grayson Griffin from the school. Grayson has always been a terrific athlete, not to mention a nice guy. It's really weird how people don't seem to change much. Boyd's been the most popular guy in every class since we started. Even in third grade, the little girls were crazy about him. Back then, I'd have simply died if one of them had a crush on me, but not Boyd. He thought it was great, and he'd be really nice to all of them. Oh, he'd tease them and all, but you could tell he always liked them."

"Were you and Boyd best friends then, too?"

"Yeah. Boyd's parents and my parents were friends before Boyd and I were born. We kind of grew up together; we're more like brothers than friends. I don't have any real brothers or sisters. When my folks split, Boyd heard the whole thing; he was always there for me. We got a lot closer that year."

"Where's your father?" Judie asked a bit timidly. She didn't want to ask too many questions, but she thought he wanted to talk.

"He's living in Kansas City. He's remarried now, and he and Terry have a son of their own. I go there in the summer for a few weeks. Jason, my half-brother, is two years old and very cute."

"I bet that's kind of neat. I've missed my brother a lot since he left home. It's been kind of hard without him. With him gone, my parents focus all their parental guidance on me."

Russ laughed. "How old is your brother?"

"Matt's twenty-two. He went to college for a while, and now he's living in my old hometown."

"Is he married?"

"No," Judie answered hesitantly, "but he's been living with this really neat woman, Dayna, for about three years. She's in optometry school, and he's working as a carpenter. They're great. I have to admit, though, I

84

wasn't too crazy about Dayna taking my brother away from me. But now, it just seems like they should be together. I'll never forget the day that I met her. Matt and I were in the back yard playing basketball on the patio, and in drives this dark-haired girl in an old red MG. It was really muddy, and when she got out of the car, Matt introduced her to me. Well, I was still in junior high, and I knew that from the way he'd talked about her, he thought she was real special, so I didn't like her. But then she took the ball from Matt, and we played for a couple of hours, the three of us. All Matt's girlfriends before Dayna were prissy and wore a lot of perfume. Anyway, by the time we stopped playing, we were all kind of muddy and I was crazy about her. She's like my big sister."

"That's really neat. I know it was tough for me to accept Terry," Russ said.

"Did your dad leave your mom for Terry?" Judie asked.

"No, as a matter of fact, my mom left my dad. They hadn't been getting along for quite a while. I wanted to stay with Mom because she was staying here. I thought about going with my dad, but really, I've always been closer to my mom. I miss him, but I see him on holidays and summers."

"I've only seen Matt once since we moved. I think it would be great if he and Dayna have kids, but they say they're not going to. I hope they change their minds, but that's easy for me to say. Being an aunt is a lot easier than being a mom or dad." Judie felt completely comfortable talking to Russ and she hoped he felt comfortable, too.

"Do you think they will change their minds? About getting married, I mean."

"Only if something changes. They don't need it.

They're happy. It did throw Mom and Dad for quite a loop for a while. They got pretty unstrung."

Russ laughed again. "I'll bet. Look, Judie, I have to do some homework, and it's my night to do the dishes, so I'd better get off the phone."

"Okay. I'm sorry I talked so much," Judie said, "but I wanted to let you know how sorry I am."

"That's okay. You sure didn't throw the first punch. Listen, I've been meaning to ask you, well, are you busy all week?"

"No," Judie said anxiously.

"How about a date tomorrow night? That's pretty short notice and a school night, to boot, but I think it would be fun. If you wanted, though, we could wait until the weekend."

"No," she said, "I think it'll be okay if I don't stay out too late."

"Great," Russ said. "Maybe we can go to the show or something. Let's see, practice lasts until six thirty, so how about seven thirty. Does that give you enough time?"

"Sure. Provided I get permission from my parents, but I'm sure they won't care."

"Okay, great. I'll see you at school tomorrow," he said.

"All right. Take it easy. Bye."

"Good night," Russ said, his voice deep and smooth, and Judie couldn't get it out of her mind.

Judie laid the receiver back on its cradle and sat down, realizing she'd been standing rigidly the entire time. "I have a date with Russ Dwyer," she squealed elatedly and then laughed out loud. This day wasn't turning out so badly after all.

Chapter Fifteen

"Tack, you've got to help," Judie said after seventh hour let out and before practice began.

"Help? With what?"

"I have a date tonight. With Russ. I'm scared to death."

"You didn't think there was anything to worry about when I was so paranoid about my first date with Sara." He grinned.

"That was different," Judie complained. "That was *you*. This is *me*."

"So, what's the difference? Except that I had to deal with meeting her parents. Girls get by easy."

"Oh, yeah? Well, guys don't have to sweat it out both ways. Girls have to worry about the guy liking her parents and her parents liking the guy. Not to mention having to sweat out not being in control."

"What do you mean 'in control'?" he asked.

"The guy drives," Judie said simply, "and he decides ultimately where you're going and when you're going home. Sure, if he's cool, the girl gets to help make the decisions, but if he turns out to be a jerk, and say he wants to park somewhere and she doesn't want to, then there's going to be a fight. And if she does want to go parking and he doesn't, then forget it. The guy gets to call all the shots." Judie reached distractedly into her locker and pulled out the ski jacket her brother gave her for her birthday.

"What about women's lib? Why don't you drive and pay his way?"

"That would be fine with me. And, by the way, don't say 'women's lib' say 'feminism.' Not having to pay is great for the girl financially, but it wouldn't bother me to pay my share or for all of it half the time. But I do think the financial reason is why so many women put up with the traditional system. It's the best part."

Tack studied Judie for a while, then said, "If you want to reduce your nervousness, then we'd better quit talking dating politics."

They walked out to Judie's car and got in. "How long before practice?" she asked.

"Twenty minutes," he said.

"Okay. Here's 'My Problem' in a nutshell. I can't picture myself dating."

"Why? Everyone goes out sometimes. You've told me yourself that you used to have a boyfriend at Bookner."

"That was different. Jeff and I had been around each other a long time, and, well, it just wasn't..."

"Sexual?" Tack asked.

Judie looked at Tack to see what expression he was wearing. No teasing there. "Well, I'm afraid about seeing Russ tonight because I just have trouble thinking of myself as a sexual being. I'm just Judie. I don't look any different to myself than I did ten years ago. Sure, I went through puberty, but it didn't flash a neon sign to me when I looked in the mirror. It didn't make me feel mature or anything. I still felt like a kid."

"Only with breasts?"

"You're making fun of me," Judie lamented, looking at him with total disappointment. She knew her face

88

was red—a definite disadvantage of her light complexion.

"No, I'm not. I swear to God, I'm not, Judie. Look at me." She did. He really wasn't making fun of her. She could trust him. "I go through the same kind of thing you're going through. I see myself as a high school kid, a son, a basketball player, a little brother, and friend. But not a lover. And definitely not a man."

"And I don't feel like a woman," Judie said. "I couldn't seduce someone. My body's not that great. And I don't think I'm ready for sex, regardless who does the seducing."

"Jude," Tack said, putting his hand on her arm, "you're not alone in that. It's scary. But I can see you as anything you want to be seen as. You can be a daughter and a friend and a ball player and still be the same person on a date. Russ is probably going through the same thing."

"But he sees me as a basketball player."

"Judie, he doesn't see you exclusively as a basketball player," Tack said, a smile breaking out across his face. "He didn't ask me out." Judie's face brightened. "And don't be afraid of getting a lot of sexual pressure from Russ. He's pretty inexperienced, too, I imagine. Like most of us."

"Are you inexperienced, Tack?" she asked, curious. "With all the dating you've been doing, I was beginning to wonder."

"Sure I am, basically. Even the guys I know who have fairly active sex lives are still inexperienced. It seems to me that unless sex is part of the whole experience, then it's not the same. It's just sex."

Judie looked at Tack intently. His face was slightly red, and he spent most of his time looking at his hands.

But she knew he was being totally honest—laying his feelings on the line—and she respected him for it.

"I hate the image most guys give off," he said. "You know, the 'I can get sex anytime I ask for it' business. They act as though women are just bodies that some guy can get sex 'off of.' Even worse, they act like high school girls who like sex are nymphomaniacs or something. That cracks me up. Why should 'nice girls' not like sex? I always hoped that someone I cared for would enjoy it as much as I did."

"Tack, you'll be a feminist yet!" Judie beamed.

He looked up and took a deep breath. "I guess I am, really. At least about the things I know about. But don't tell my brother Chris. He'd kill me if he heard me say that."

"Never mind your brother," Judie said, looking at Tack's watch. "I'm back to panicking. It's easy for me to see you as a sexual person, just not me. You're gentle and you have wonderful eyes. Like Timothy Hutton."

Tack opened the car door, then said, "We'd better start walking back before we're late and I get embarrassed. Thanks for the compliment. And I might as well tell you that I think you're really beautiful. I always have. Since the first practice. You've got what it takes inside and out, Conklin." He got out and slammed the car door. "And I'm not the only one. I've heard several guys comment about various features you have. I don't care how long you pester me, I'm not telling who had dibs on what body part."

Judie tried to hide her confusion. "It seems a little weird talking about this stuff with you, but not too weird."

"Yeah," Tack said, "it feels all right."

Judie played well in practice that day, unlike the

day before, but she didn't speak to Russ at all, nor he to her. "Neither of us knows what to say," she whispered to Tack. "We're both ignoring 'the big date.'"

After the coach blew the final whistle at six fifteen, Russ walked over to Judie. "Still on for tonight?" he asked.

"Sure," Judie replied, "see you at seven thirty. Do you know my address?"

"Yes. I've driven by a couple of times hoping to catch you outside. Coincidentally, of course."

"Well, I guess I'll see you a little later." Judie grabbed her warm-ups and headed for the showers.

When she got home, she went straight to her bedroom to start getting ready. Her mother asked her if she wanted dinner, but Judie didn't feel like eating. Besides, she told her mother, she wasn't sure if Russ planned to take her to eat or not. Her mother smiled sweetly and shook her head. It irritated Judie that her mother was so happy about her date. She hadn't even wanted to tell her about it.

At seven twenty-five Judie heard the doorbell ring; she knew it was Russ. She heard her father trying to make some glad-to-meet-you conversation, which, with her father, inevitably led to professional sports. She hurried so Russ wouldn't be trapped too long. Judie took a brief glance in the mirror. She was happy with her complexion—very few pimples—but wished for a different color hair—strawberry blond—hair that wasn't blond or auburn, but somewhere in between. I should've gotten it cut last week, she thought anxiously. And her fingernails—her basketball playing fingers—looked practical but unappealing. Amy Denniston had long, polished fingernails. Was she dressed too casually? Her mother thought so. But Levi's were her style, and she didn't want him to think she'd gotten all dressed up.

But there was a definite problem with Levi's; your waist/inseam was emblazoned right there on your ass. Am I too tall and thin? Willowy didn't seem to be in....

"Judie," her mother called, "Russ is here."

"You'll just have to do, Conklin," she muttered softly.

Russ stood up when she walked into the room. It was more of a let's-get-out-of-here kind of stand up than one of politeness.

"We'll be home early," she heard herself tell her parents.

"It was nice meeting you both," Russ said in a nervous voice.

"It was nice meeting you, too, Russ," her mother said. "Judie's told us a lot about you." Judie shot her mother a "don't overdo" look.

"I look forward to seeing you play again this week, Russ. Those Cougars have a tough job ahead of them if they think they can beat you guys," her father said. Judie forgave him for being his usual overzealous self. She knew that he just wanted to make Russ feel good, hokey or not.

"Good night," everyone chimed in no particular order, and it seemed to Judie that everyone said it more than once just to make sure that no one was left unanswered. Judie smirked at the absurdity of the entire episode. First dates were always murder.

"They're pretty nice," Russ said once they were both in the car.

"Yeah. My dad tries awfully hard, but sometimes he comes off a little sappy."

Russ reached down to turn on the radio. "What kind of music do you like? I'm big on jazz."

"I'm more into folk rock, but I like good jazz, too. I am really pretty ignorant about it though."

The conversation flowed easily enough, but Judie

hated all the non-personal topics. They had talked more in-depth over the phone yesterday, but tonight, they were like total strangers. Even when they talked about basketball, they kept an unnatural distance.

"Hungry?" Russ asked.

"Not really. But if you want to get something, it's okay with me."

"No, I've already eaten, but I realized that we never made any plans about dinner. I just wanted to make sure that you weren't starving."

"Russ, it's kind of crazy how stiff this feels, isn't it? I mean you're afraid that I might not have eaten, and I'm afraid that it's really you who's hungry."

"Yeah," Russ said, relaxing a little. "It feels sort of like a *date*." They both laughed heartily. "And the biggest reason I wanted to take you out was because we seemed to have something in common and it's easy for me to talk to you. Unlike Boyd, I have trouble talking to girls."

"I guess I don't seem like a girl," Judie tested. The worries she'd expressed to Tack were coming back quickly.

"You're definitely a girl, it's just that I've been around you more, and you seem real. You have a good sense of humor, and you're easy to talk to. I guess I'm rambling, huh?" He looked at Judie expectantly, then shrugged. "I'm not saying it right—but I promise, it's a compliment."

"Thanks, Russ."

They drove on in silence until he asked her what movie she wanted to see.

"Since we're making this seem like a date, I'll just say 'I don't care' and 'Why don't you pick?'"

"Then I can counter with 'No, you pick.' That way

we can stall around long enough to miss the movie and have nothing to do."

They laughed again, and Russ reached across the seat and put his hand on her knee. "You're pretty neat, Judie," he said. "Is *Ordinary People* okay with you?"

"Sure. I'm going to break another date rule, though, and admit that I've seen it. I've seen it twice, but I love it, and I'd like to see it again."

"Great," Russ said, "because I've seen it already, too. I think it's a wonderful movie."

The movie started just as they were getting popcorn. "Go on in and save us some seats," Russ insisted. "Is Coke all right?"

"Fine," she said. Judie found two seats about halfway back in the center section and sat down. It was getting easier all the time.

After the movie was over, they relived a few scenes on the way out to the car. "Have you read the book?" Judie asked.

"No," he answered.

"If you want, I'll bring it to you. It's really good."

"Is it much different from the movie?" he asked. "I hate it when I really like one version, so I either read the book or see the movie, whichever I haven't yet done, and it differs so much that I don't like it."

"Well," Judie began, "the book was first, so it deserves a read. But it is different some. For instance, there's a lot more of a relationship between Conrad and Jeanine."

"That's good. I thought that there needed to be more in the movie. Good grief, I mean, they're our age and all they do is go to McDonald's and hold hands. It's pretty unrealistic."

"Yes," Judie said, "that's true." She was beginning to feel uncomfortable talking about relationships.

When they got to the car, Russ opened her door for her. She tried to tell herself it was because the door was locked and he didn't want her standing in the cold while he reached across the car seat, but still she wasn't too crazy about the idea. She was angry with herself for not saying anything.

"What time is it?" Russ asked. "I forgot my watch."

"About ten o'clock," she answered.

"Well, I'd better get you home. I'd hate for your parents to think I was a bad influence on you for keeping you out on a school night."

Judie sensed that he was a little nervous, and when they got to her house, Russ left the car running as he got out of the car and hurried around to open Judie's door.

"I can get it," she said.

"Oh," he said, looking back at the car. "Can I walk you to the door?"

"Sure," she said, "I'd like that." She looked at him, then took his arm.

When they reached the porch, Judie waited for her mother to stick her head out or for her father to turn on the porch lights, but neither happened. When she smiled to herself, Russ asked why she was smiling.

She told him. "I guess I watch too many sit-com reruns," she said.

He put his arms around her, and slowly leaned down and kissed her tenderly. Jeff never kissed like this, she thought.

"Good night, Judie," he said. "I'd like to see you again." He looked at her without blinking, and those brown eyes worked like magnets.

"Me, too," she said, pulling his face down toward her. She kissed him again before going inside.

* * *

"Who in the world could that be?" her father half yelled as he tied the sash of his bathrobe and made his way past Judie in the dark hallway.

Judie wrapped herself in the quilt she slept under and followed her father to the door—the doorbell had woken them all. She looked around for her mother and caught a glimpse of her heading toward the bathroom, taking her curlers out as she walked. Her father opened the door as far as the chain allowed, said, "It's you!", slammed the door shut, and unlatched the chain. He opened the door and hugged the body standing there. Judie had to walk closer just to see who it was.

"Judie!" Dayna said as she unwound from the embrace and reached to hug Judie.

"Where's Matthew?" her father asked, now completely awake.

"He should be coming in soon; he was trying to find his camera when I left him by the car." Dayna walked into the living room and looked around. "So this is it, huh? It's nice. We barely found this place, and we stopped and asked directions at a gas station and everything. No luck. Finally, somehow, we got on Heitman Street, so we followed it across town, and here we are."

Judie sat down on the couch and looked at her almost-sister-in-law. "You look great, Dayna," she said.

"So do you," she said, smiling as she rubbed her hands together for warmth.

Matt walked through the door as his mother entered the room. "You didn't have to take your curlers out for me, Ma," he said, laughing the laugh that made Judie get up and walk over to him.

"It's so good to see you," Judie told him, reaching for him.

"It's good to see you, baby. How's life treating you?"

he asked as he put his camera equipment down and hugged their mother.

Before Judie could answer, Rose Conklin interrupted. "You've grown a beard!" she yelled.

"At least that's what *he* calls it. I say it's more of a 'growth' than a real beard." Dayna laughed her deep laugh, and Judie followed suit. "Matt and I decided yesterday that it had been too long since we've seen you. *Voilà*." She looked at Judie and then at the others, and Judie thought that it was just like the two of them to take off and drive to see them without any warning or hoopla planned.

"You could've given me a chance to get this place in order before you saw it for the first time. It's a mess—not good for your first impression," their mother said, shaking her head.

Judie suppressed a giggle when she noticed her brother assume his "dutiful son" role. "It's a terrific house, Ma. I love the hardwood floors and the little bay window upstairs."

"How could you see it in the dark? Let me give you the grand tour. You should be designing houses like this one, Matt. You've always been so good at that sort of thing."

"Building houses interests me. You know I'm not interested in architecture. You should know that by now." He looked at her with disgust.

"Okay, I promise to be good," she apologized. "But let me show you the house." She took him by the hand and led him up the stairway.

"Anyone care for coffee? I think I'll make some if anyone else could stand a cup." Joe Conklin looked around the room for reactions. "Dayna?"

"Please," she said. After he had disappeared into the

kitchen, she turned her attention to Judie. "So's how's basketball?"

"The game itself is fine. That part is always good."

"And other parts?"

Judie smiled and shrugged. "I guess it could be better. Occasionally it really gets to me, but usually I'm okay." Judie knew that Dayna wouldn't let her off the hook so easily, but she really didn't know how to answer her without taking all night.

"Do you like school? Everything going okay?"

"Yeah. All in all."

"Good. And what about that guy?" Dayna asked.

Judie didn't know if she was talking about Tack or Russ, but she assumed from the look in Dayna's eye—that you-can-tell-me look—that she meant Russ. "I'd forgotten I told you about him over the phone. We went out last night. I had fun, but it's scary."

Dayna smiled again and nodded her head. "Matt scared me sometimes. Or our relationship did—and it still does often enough. But the only thing you can count on is that you can't count on anything ever finally being settled. You have to constantly work on relationships—there isn't a point at which you can stop and say, 'Well, we've done it; it's smooth sailing from here on out.' That only happens on television."

Judie's father came out with a tray of coffee and cups. "Soup's on," he interrupted, happy to please Dayna.

"Is there enough for us?" Matt asked as they descended the stairs.

"Sure," he said, though Judie thought she caught a note of disappointment that he wasn't going to be able to talk to Dayna alone. As they sat around drinking coffee and talking small talk, Judie thought about what Dayna had said. She and Matt never fought; they

98

seemed the perfect couple. Judie wondered how long they dated before they started sleeping together; she decided to ask Dayna if she got a chance. It wasn't a topic easily worked into conversations around the Conklin dinner table.

Soon the group started to disperse, and Judie was shocked by her mother's directions that the two could use the guest room. Though Judie knew her mother understood that they had been living together for a long time, it still surprised her that she didn't have Matt sleep on the couch. Judie caught Matt's eye, and he winked at her. "Where do you keep the sheets?" he asked his mother.

"The bed's already made," she said, picking up the tray, then looking back up and smiling. "It's good to have you here," she said. "When do you have to go back?"

"Thursday night," Matt said. "Dayna has an exam Friday."

Their mother shook her head up and down, wishing they could stay longer. Judie felt good; she really missed seeing Matt and Dayna on a weekly—often daily—basis. What used to be Matt's place in her heart was really now Matt and Dayna's place. Judie knew that if she had to choose between them—a game she and Matt played when they were little—that she would choose Matt because he was her brother and Dayna was not. But she was damned close.

As she started to get in bed, she realized she'd left her quilt downstairs, and though she had plenty of other blankets, she liked the way that one felt on her, so she went to get it. On her way down the stairs, she was surprised to hear voices; everyone started toward their bedrooms when she had. She froze on the stairs when she heard her name being shouted in the conversation.

"It's her life!" Matt's voice yelled. "You don't have any right to interfere with it. And to tell you the truth, that's the real reason we're here. For God's sake, somebody has to give her some support, and it's obvious you don't!"

Judie turned and headed back upstairs without the quilt. As she passed the guest room, she looked in and saw Dayna digging around in her suitcase, and then pulling back the covers on the bed.

"Good night, Dayna," she said.

"Night."

Judie went on into her own room and got in bed, thinking of how nice it must feel to go to sleep holding on to someone you really loved.

Chapter Sixteen

Just as Judie slammed the door shut on Tack's Mustang, Tack asked her how the date went.

"Fine," she said. "I had a good time."

"That's good," Tack said. They rode along in silence for a few blocks, then simultaneously began to speak.

"Go ahead," Tack said.

"Matt and Dayna surprised us with a visit this week is all—it'll hold."

"I was just going to ask you if Russ invited you to homecoming."

"No," Judie replied. "I hadn't even really thought about it."

"The reason I asked is because I think he's already taking Amy Denniston."

Judie looked out the passenger window; she hadn't considered the possibility of Russ having another date this weekend. "Well, if you thought that, why'd you ask me if he'd invited me to homecoming?"

"Sorry," Tack said sarcastically, "I just thought if he asked you, then obviously he hadn't asked Amy. No big deal."

Judie didn't talk the rest of the way to school. She thought about Russ and why he didn't tell her he had a date for homecoming. Why should he tell me? she thought. I don't have any hold over him. Still, she couldn't deny she was hurt. All the good she felt about the night before was vanishing; she could never compete with "National Velvet" Amy, the perfect cheerleader.

"Hey," Tack said on the way into the building, "are you in a trance or what?"

"Yeah. I'm zombied out."

"Too many drugs?" he kidded.

"Definitely," Judie said. "Just like my grandmother always says, 'Those hippie high school kids are all high on drugs.'"

Tack laughed willingly. Judie could tell he felt uneasy when she was the least bit depressed. "My grandparents all say 'high on drugs' too. Not just 'high' or 'on drugs' but both. It's kind of redundant, don't you think?"

"Who are you taking to homecoming, Tack? Sara?"

"No," he said hesitantly. "Ellen Todd."

"What happened to Sara?" Judie asked tauntingly.

"Give me a break," he said, "it just didn't work out." Tack walked on to his locker without waiting for Judie to get her books for first hour. Cassie asked Judie if she and Tack were fighting.

"No, why?"

"Well," Cassie said, "I've heard that Sara wouldn't go with him to homecoming because she was jealous of you."

"Of me? That's crazy. It doesn't make sense."

"Sure it does, Judie. Sara didn't like being treated like second string. She says he talks about you constantly."

"But that's because we're best friends. We're together all the time, so no wonder he talks about me."

Cassie shrugged her shoulders. "I understand, Judie, but I don't think Sara wanted to understand. It took me forever to finally believe you. I think she told Tack that it bothered her, and he said that he wasn't going to change. Anyway, they're not going to homecoming together."

"Did I hear that Tack hasn't asked anyone to homecoming?" Ann asked, as she walked up to the others carrying her books. Ann was slightly overweight, but she always looked good in clothes she chose.

"No," Judie answered, "he's taking Ellen Todd."

"Rats," Ann said, "another possibility down the drain."

"So, do you have a date?" Cassie asked Judie. "I hear you and Russ went out last night."

"News sure gets around. No, he didn't ask me to homecoming. I think he's taking Amy Denniston," Judie said, trying to be nonchalant.

"I hope not. She's so damned..."

"Peppy," Ann chimed in.

"Good word," Cassie said, smiling. "So, did the date go okay?"

"Yes. I had a good time. We went to *Ordinary People.*"

"Haven't you seen that?"

"Twice," Judie said, "but we both wanted to see it again."

"So, does Russ care about Tack?" Ann asked.

Judie gave them both disgusted stares. "You guys are too much. Of course he doesn't care about Tack. He knows we're just friends."

"But he's a nice, funny, good-looking guy. That makes a difference to me, and I'm sure it does to Russ. Those blue eyes of Tack's can't be ignored," Cassie said.

"Well," Ann said, "if I were you, I'd drop Russ like a hot potato and try my damnedest to make all those rumors about you and Tack true. I think he's an absolute doll."

They all laughed, but Judie felt uneasy. She found Tack attractive too, but she knew that he thought of her as his best friend.

"Are you sure you guys are just friends?" Ann teased her after catching Judie's almost embarrassed expression. "No post-game work-outs?"

Judie shook her head, but couldn't help laughing at Ann's suggestions. "He's like a brother," she said, trying to make her friends believe in their platonic relationship.

"Sounds incestuously delicious to me," Ann said.

The hilarity was cut short by the sounding of the first bell. As they were walking off to class, Russ stopped at Judie's locker, and Judie's heart started pounding faster. She knew her face was red from the kidding she'd been getting, and for some reason, it seemed important that Russ not find out what they'd been kidding her about.

"Can I walk you?" he asked, pointing down the hallway with the corner of his textbook.

"Sure," she said, "but you make it sound like you're walking your dog."

"How do you come up with lines like that so fast? I swear you crack me up." When he looked at her this time, it was different. He glanced at her hair and moved his gaze down her body so slowly that it made her feel naked.

"I forgot to tell you last night," he began, "and I want to tell you before you hear it from someone else."

"I already know," she murmured. "You're taking Amy to homecoming."

"How did you know?" He sighed, his voice full of regret.

"I heard it from several people," she said. No sense

in saving his feelings. He might as well hurt a little, too.

"Well," he said, "although it's no consolation, I just wanted to tell you that Boyd set it up a long time ago. We're doubling with him and Trish Owen."

"Russ," Judie said, not liking the way he spoke—as if he were crushing her by not taking her to homecoming, "it's not that big a deal."

"Okay," he said, taking her arm to swing her so they were facing each other, "but I just want to say that, well, that I wish I was going with you."

Judie felt a flitter in her stomach and her manner softened. "Thanks, Russ. That's really nice."

"So how about Saturday night?" he asked. "Will you go out with me Saturday night?"

"Sure. What time?"

"Eight?"

"Eight's fine."

"And though it's traditional to take your homecoming date to the parade on Thursday night, will you go with me instead?"

"What about Amy? Won't that hurt her feelings?" Judie asked.

"I've already told her that I wanted to take you. I think she's a little upset about it, but I'm sure someone else will be happy to step in. I would never have asked her out if Boyd hadn't stepped in. He just doesn't understand that we have different tastes sometimes." He looked at Judie. "Thursday, then?"

"Thursday," she said. "Wait, Tack and I have already made plans to go together." She waited for Russ to say that the three of them could make an evening of it.

"Can you get out of it?" he asked.

"Well," Judie said, caught off guard, "I guess I could."

"Great," he said, "pick you up at, say, five thirty.

We'll only have a short practice that day." He leaned down and kissed Judie's cheek, then sped off to class. Judie, standing alone in the middle of a busy hallway, felt like the young damsel in some old movie, in a state of bewildered gaiety, but oddly out of control.

That afternoon, Matt got her out of her last class. "When does your practice start?" he asked.

"Not until three forty-five. We've got an hour. What do you have in mind?"

He shrugged. "I just wanted to spend some time with you before we go back, and we're leaving tomorrow afternoon while you're still in practice."

Judie got her jacket from her locker, and she felt a sudden pang of sadness. "I wish you didn't have to leave..." she began.

"Maybe you can come down over spring break," he said, stroking his beard nervously, careful not to look at her. When their eyes met, though, the tension broke and he smiled. "I guess we can spend a little time feeling lousy. I'm going to miss you, too." He clasped his hands together, then his "take-charge" self took over. "What can you show me in this town before I leave? So far I haven't seen or done anything."

Judie tried to think of something to show him, but couldn't. "I guess we could just drive around and see the town. Not much there, though." She motioned for him to follow her toward the parking lot, then stopped. "I'd like for you to meet someone, but we'll have to be a little crafty to get him out of class."

"How about if I tell the teacher that I'm his older brother come home to visit. How's that?"

Judie smiled. "That should work. I hope we don't get him in trouble." They started walking toward the art classroom where Tack was, and once they got there Matt's plan worked.

"Tack, this is my brother, Matt. And Matt, this is my friend, Tack Cienelli." Judie had a funny feeling in her stomach as they shook hands. Tack looked handsome wearing his blue and gray sweater, but Judie noticed that he seemed a little nervous as he tried to make small talk with Matt. Tack was just about the same height as Matt, but Matt looked a little more self-assured, and Judie tried to read Matt's face to see if he liked Tack. Somehow it was very important they liked each other, and when silence descended, Judie panicked.

"We've got to run," she said to Tack nonsensically, taking Matt's arm.

"Nice to meet you," Matt said somewhat perplexed.

"You, too," Tack said, turning to go back to class.

When Judie and Matt reached his car, he said, "He's nice enough, I guess, though I'm afraid I'll never be too crazy about your boyfriends."

When Judie explained that Tack wasn't her boyfriend, she wasn't sure that Matt believed her. The topic was soon exhausted however when she finally took Matt out to a place a few miles out of town Tack had shown her not long after the season started.

"There's a little waterfall that runs here in the summertime," Judie explained. "Now that it's dry, we can search for Indian arrowheads."

"Have you found some?" Matt asked.

"I haven't, but Tack has four or five that he's collected from here since he was little. Mostly we come out here just to talk; the arrowhead-hunting is just something to do while we talk."

"Sounds kind of like what I wanted to do," Matt said, as he shoved his hands deeper in his pockets and stared at the mixture of shale and flint rocks that made up the bed. "What do they look like anyway? In case I'm staring at one and don't know it."

"Well, the ones Tack has are about an inch or two long and not very thick. And they're usually gray," she said, thinking back to the ones she'd seen. "They really look like arrowheads, only usually they've been chipped from age. Tack says that this was a big hang-out back then, and not for just one tribe. A lot of little towns around here have Indian tribal names. Tack is big on history."

They walked around until Judie had to go back for basketball practice, talking about school and their hometown and basketball. But the part Judie liked best was having him tell her about the troubles he had had with their parents that she didn't know about. "You were just a kid then," he said reflectively. "You couldn't have understood any better than they could understand."

"But they could have understood if they'd tried," Judie said defensively. "They just didn't, just like they're not trying now for me." They walked the long way back to the car through the woods where the trees looked naked. "I wished you could've seen this place about a month or so ago. The colors of the leaves were just incredible."

Matt smiled, then pulled Judie close. They walked on, holding each other, without talking. "I know it's tough," he said as he shut his car door, then rubbed his hands together for warmth, "but you know Mom's just a little old-fashioned. It's hard for her to accept you and basketball, but I think she's coming around some." He looked over at her as he pulled back on the road. "Slowly, but surely."

When Judie got out of the car at the gym, she walked over to the driver's side and motioned for Matt to roll down his window. She leaned in and kissed his cheek, and she thought he might cry. "Have a good trip," she said. "And thanks, Matt. You're terrific."

He winked, then sped away. Judie buttoned her coat, and went in to find Tack.

Chapter Seventeen

"Make it count out there your first quarter, Judie," the coach said during warm-ups, "that's all you're going to play."

"What are you talking about?" she asked. Not only was this the homecoming game, which itself almost doubled the size of the crowd, but Coleman High had one of the toughest B teams in the conference.

"I'm saving you for the varsity. You know the rules. If you only play one quarter of B-team ball, you're still eligible during the varsity game. It's that simple."

Judie jogged back out to warm-up. Her mind raced while she sank her first few baskets. Big crowd, her first varsity appearance. Russ and Amy. After last night at the parade, she was sure that he really didn't want to go with Amy tonight, but if anyone could change his mind, Judie was sure Amy could. She looked around to see where Amy was. She wasn't cheering yet; she was a varsity cheerleader. But she had to be here somewhere. After all, her date was playing on the B team. She spotted Amy in the stands talking to Boyd. Damned Boyd; he was always trying to get Russ to "broaden his horizons" a little.

"Hey," Russ said, "what was the coach saying to you?"

"I'm only going to play a quarter, and then I'm suiting out for the varsity game." Russ looked at her blankly. "I probably won't get to play any," she placated.

"Probably not," Russ said.

Judie was angry with herself for minimizing playing for the varsity just to soothe Russ's ego, but she was more angry with him for showing it. She stared at him irritably.

"Tack's trying to get your attention," he said sharply.

"I'm sure he's thrilled."

"At least that makes two of us," she said, turning her back on Russ.

"I hear you're suiting up. Great!" Tack said.

"Yeah, but I don't get it. Do you have any idea why?"

"Bruce Connors is having trouble with his knee again. His doctor is threatening to make him have surgery right away if it doesn't heal. And chances are it won't heal unless he stays off it some." Tack shook Judie's hand. "So you're moving up to the Major League—for the time being, anyway."

The buzzer sounded. As Judie made her way back to the sidelines for the huddle, Russ whispered, "I'm sorry. You'll do great," and he winked at her.

Judie played well during the first quarter, and for the first time, she and Franky began to connect on court. It was like they were trying to one-up each other, and as a result, were playing terrific basketball. Russ was having a poor game, though, and the coach sent Brondel in for him. When the quarter ended, Meier was ahead by eight. Judie figured that since she and Franky were doing so well, the coach would likely leave them alone, especially in light of the fact that they were predicted to lose, and a win could go far in boosting their image. But, as planned, the coach took Judie out of the game. He handed her a varsity uniform on her way out, and she felt proud.

Judie had to walk down to freshmen hall to use the girls' gym class facilities, but it was better than nothing. She wanted to cool off before putting on the better quality, more prestigious garment. When she noticed the number on her uniform, she laughed out loud. The perfect symbol for a maverick: number 13.

She would have to put her B-team sweats back on over the varsity uniform, but it seemed of little consequence as she looked at herself in the mirror. Her hair looked more blond than strawberry against the red, and when she pulled it back, she finally believed she was playing varsity ball. Not that she looked like a boy—she didn't—but she looked capable. Her legs were long, lean and strong, and she felt at her physical peak. As she stared at her image, she wished she had time to put a few darts in the new jersey, but it didn't fit too loosely. She suddenly realized that she liked the way she looked. She wasn't a girl in a boy's uniform, but a Meier player—different but not wrong. She smiled and gave herself an "okay" sign, then left.

Before she reached the lobby packed with people wanting soft drinks and popcorn, Judie felt herself stop. She sat down on the concrete floor and waited for the buzzer to send the second half on its way. Sitting there in the dark, she felt sort of like an outlaw.

She wondered what the score was. The coach probably put in Nick Danschenko to replace her. It was the first time all season he'd gotten much of a chance to play, and in a couple of years, he'd make a decent guard. She wished Tack was with her so they could talk, but there was no way to get his attention without getting everyone's.

The noise in the lobby began to die down, and Judie peered around the hallway to see if she was right, and she was. She walked to the concession stand and found out the score from the attendant: 28–26, Coleman's lead. "He's probably letting the guard break up the middle," she thought.

Tack was nowhere in sight, and Judie figured that the varsity players were already dressing. She sat in the northeast section of the gym behind some junior high kids, where she would draw as little attention to herself as possible.

Nick wasn't playing any longer; Mike Dale had taken his place. Mike was getting suckered into the same mistakes Nick had made, and Judie could tell what the problem was. Franky was yelling and screaming at Mike.

Poor Franky, she thought. It must be hard on him knowing that they could use me. Russ was doing better now. Because she wasn't playing? She didn't know. He was back to being the same old steady Russ: never flashy, and never the best player on the court. He'd have trouble making the varsity next year since Phil Derrick was the only senior forward graduating.

Judie spotted Tack coming into the gym, and he was searching for her. Though she waved a few times, he didn't see her. She made her way down to see him.

"Judie," a woman's voice said.

Judie turned, and there sat her mother and father. "What are you doing here?" she asked excitedly.

"Trying to watch you play. What happened?"

"I'm suiting out for the varsity," she said with pride.

"That's my girl!" Her father beamed.

"Congratulations, dear," her mother said.

"Well," Judie said, "I've got to run. Tack's waiting for me."

She left them feeling a little happier. Tack hugged her when she reached him. "I'm so proud of you," he said. "We're sitting on the bench together now; next year we'll be the starting guards of Meier High."

"Don't count your chickens," Judie said, feigning a nonchalance.

The B-team game ended as they were talking. As Judie expected, Meier lost, and she could see Franky leave the court, muttering near-profanities and gesturing wildly. "I feel sort of sorry for Franky," she said to Tack.

He looked at her. "I can understand that," he replied. "He played a hell of a game."

"That's not why. Not because they lost, but because he wanted to show everyone so badly that the B team could do without me."

"And the coach picked you to suit out with the varsity instead of him," Tack added. He put his arm around her shoulder, "But you're the only person I know who could really pity him," he said, looking at her intensely. When she glanced at him, he broke off his stare, embarrassed. "So did you and Russ have a good time last night?"

"Yeah, we had a lot of fun," Judie answered, feeling like a traitor for breaking her plans with Tack. "I'm really sorry about cutting you off with such short notice."

"Well, now we're even. Besides, I think Ellen thought I was a little bit crazy for not asking her to the parade when we have a date for homecoming. So, I asked her at the last minute, and we had a good time. She's a nice person."

"Nice person? That doesn't sound like the Tack I know. No from-the-heart pet names?"

Tack turned a little red. "So she's not girl-of-my-dreams material. We'll have a good enough time."

"Is something wrong, Tack? You sound kind of down."

"I can't talk about it here. But, yeah, I'm kind of down about women. I just lose interest in them after a couple of dates. They just don't measure up somehow."

"Measure up to what?"

Tack rubbed his chin. "That's what I can't figure out. I'm crazy about them before we go out, and maybe for the first date or so, but not after that. I think I'm weird."

"Let's talk about it."

"How about tonight?" Tack asked. "After I take Ellen home? I could drive over around eleven thirty or so, okay?"

Judie thought about it for a minute. She'd probably sit around her house and worry about Russ and Amy and whether they were having a terrific time. She'd probably be sleepy by then, but she knew she would want to talk, especially to Tack. "Okay," she said, "see you then."

Judie felt strange warming up with the varsity. Of the ten players, she was the shortest. She tried not to look downcourt at the opposition because she thought she heard them snickering. The crowd didn't respond as she was afraid they might, but she was sure that if she played, they would boo her, full force.

Grayson lined up behind Judie in lay-up formation, and he whispered that she would do fine. Grayson was so self-confident sometimes that Judie thought he wasn't really a human being. He didn't seem like a high school kid. He was kind, talented, modest, friendly, and handsome—not the basic high school jock. The afternoon after what Tack called "Horrible Monday," Grayson kept telling her to take it easy, and he was genuinely hostile to Franky. Then again, he was always a little hostile to Franky; Franky was the epitome of what Grayson despised.

"Bruce is having a lot of trouble with his knee," Tack said, half worried. As soon as Bruce told the coach to bench him, Tack would take his place. Judie could tell that Tack was worried, but she also knew that he was looking forward to playing. He didn't try to hide his emotions at all, unlike Grayson. Judie smiled when she thought about how well she could read Tack.

"So I'm a little nervous," he said, comprehending her knowing smile.

The coach called them in for some last minute instructions. Judie listened carefully and anxiously, but she doubted that she would play. When the announcer called the names of the starting five, Judie felt her skin tighten as though she had stepped into a tub of too-hot water. She sat on the very end of the bench, and Tack sat next to her. They didn't say a word; they watched the game intently, hoping to get some insight should either of them play.

Grayson brought the ball down the court with a grace that Judie envied. He was easily the best guard in the conference, and maybe the state. Though the coach would never admit it, Grayson was more than just the leading scorer; he was the team's captain and the driving force behind the team's flawless record. He had the most assists, the fewest fouls, and easily the most respect of any player on the team. Judie and Tack studied him, to learn his tactics, absorb his know-how, and copy his finesse.

The team won by twelve points, and Tack played only a fleeting three minutes of the entire game. Judie didn't play at all. Once, during warm-ups for the second half, Judie peered into the stands and saw Russ sitting with Amy, and though she wasn't sure, Judie thought they were holding hands. She didn't look again.

Chapter Eighteen

When Judie got home that night, her parents accommodatingly left her alone. She tried listening to her stereo, but she couldn't stay still that long. She tried to watch TV, but it was worthless. So, she grabbed a basketball and went into the back yard to practice.

It was hard to practice dribbling on ground still frozen from last week's snow. There was a small slab of concrete near the steps, so she alternated between practicing her dribbling there and shooting baskets. She arrived home around ten o'clock and when she started playing, the time got away from her.

"Let your old dad try his luck," her father said, startling her. She looked at him, all bundled up, standing in the cold, and she thought he was beginning to look old. She smiled at him, and threw him the ball. He put up a shot, but it just hit the rim and bounced back to where he was standing. He made the second basket.

"I wish you'd gotten to play in the varsity game," he said. "That Connors boy was obviously having trouble with his knee, and it hurt us."

"Yeah," Judie said, "but it's his last season, so the coach lets him play when he's feeling all right." She shot a couple of baskets while he stood there, just watching her. She wanted to be able to say something to him, but she couldn't think of anything besides basketball to discuss.

"Remember that time when you and Matt were little—you were about eight and Matt was in junior high—and the two of you were playing one-on-one and I refereed?"

"Yeah. I wanted so badly to beat him. Looking back, I guess it was sort of impossible since he must have been about a foot taller than I was." She thought about what a treat it had been when her father would play with them—he was usually too busy or too tired from being so busy. But when he did play with them, she always wanted to show him how good she was.

"I remember I thought once that you were going to win," he said softly. "But Matt tried a little harder once he realized you were really a threat." He shrugged.

Judie said, "I loved it when you played with us."

"I wish I had done it more often," he said, glancing at her, then looking at the ground.

Judie figured that she should say something. The right thing. She wanted to make him feel better, but she didn't know how. "You taught me how to twirl the ball on my finger like Meadowlark Lemmon," she said, showing him she could still do it.

He laughed. "You always did that better than Matt did, and it used to really make him mad. I did teach you that, didn't I?"

"You sure did, Dad. Right before my ninth birthday. I showed everyone at my party."

"Was I at that party?" he asked.

"Yes," she lied. "I remember."

"Good." He started rubbing his arms, then said, "Well, Rose'll wonder what happened to me. I better go on in."

"Good night," Judie said, walking over to the concrete.

"And Judie?" her father yelled.

118

"Yeah?" she said, looking back at him.

"You're a good daughter. And a good basketball player. I'm very proud of you." He blew her a kiss, then shoved his hands deep in his pockets before heading inside.

She started her dribbling exercises—first the right hand then the left—that Coach Mickes taught her when she was just a freshman. When she really got into practicing, or playing for that matter, she had intense concentration. If she could do that when she studied for exams, she'd be a genius by now. She felt a rhythm when she played, though it wasn't like dancing. It was more from within—dancing was external. When she had tried to explain it to Tack, he had laughed and said she must have reached some sort of altered state of consciousness. "I guess I'm addicted," she had replied. She didn't really think it was far from the truth.

"Hey," Tack said softly in deference to her sleeping parents. "Sorry I'm a little late. Ellen wanted to stop for something to drink."

"I didn't even hear you drive up," she said. "Did you park on the street?"

He pointed to his car, which was in the driveway not fifty feet away. "You must have been really concentrating on your playing."

"I've gotten some good work in." Judie had long since abandoned the outer sweatshirt, and the sweatshirt she was wearing was dripping. She wanted to take it off, too, but standing around in a T-shirt in this weather would be suicidal.

Tack took the basketball and sat on the hood of his car. She sat next to Tack. "Did you get depressed tonight?" he asked. "I would've," he said, "and I did, sort of. Get depressed, I mean."

"What about?"

"Well," he began, "it's just that I feel alone some-times when I'm on a date. Like I'm on stage for her benefit. I just wish I could be myself like I am with you."

"There's no reason why you shouldn't be. Tack, the girls you have gone out with are nice people. They're regular human beings. In fact, they're probably wishing you would be just yourself."

"And they don't understand about you." Tack sighed, exasperated. "If I talk about you, then they get para-noid. Or insulted. I tried to make Sara understand, but she wouldn't listen. She said—well, never mind. It's not important."

Although Judie was curious about what Sara had said, she didn't press Tack. They sat quiet for a while. Judie felt choked by the silence, and they looked at each other intensely, both wishing that the other would climb the wall between them.

Finally, Tack spoke. "Russ told me that he really wished you were at the dance. He and Amy don't get along well," Tack said in a weak voice. "It's really neat how you guys get along so well."

"Yeah, it's kind of surprising. But I have to admit, sitting here alone tonight wasn't any fun."

"I know the feeling," Tack commented. "Well, I'd better go. I don't want to get you in trouble." He got in his car and started it without revving the engine. He waved slightly and backed out of the driveway.

Judie picked up her basketball and waved good-bye to Tack. She walked back in the house, quietly, in order not to wake her parents. One thing she didn't need right now was a heart-to-heart talk with her mother.

As she got into bed, Judie started thinking about Tack and Russ. She was anxious about her date to-morrow night; would she have to make any decisions about sex? After the parade, she and Russ sat outside her house in his car and kissed a long time. She liked the way his body felt against hers, the way he moved his hands along her body, but she had been afraid that one of her parents or a neighbor kid would walk by.

And Russ had been afraid, too. They talked a little while about how vulnerable they felt. "I just don't want us to feel uncomfortable," he said. "I want it to feel right." She remembered exactly how his voice sounded and how his face looked as he spoke last night.

She dozed off to sleep and awoke in the middle of the night; her digital clock blinked three seventeen. The dream that woke her was pounding away at her chest, and she was sweating. Her body was throbbing and her mouth was dry. She'd had dreams like this before, fantasy dreams, as Tack called them, but this one startled her. It was about Tack.

Judie felt a little awkward that night with Russ after the movie. He drove around for a long time, talking about what a miserable time he had the night before.

"So did I," Judie reminded him. "I was pretty nervous about the thought of playing, too," she said, not caring if his ego hurt a little.

"I'll bet," he said sweetly. "I'd be absolutely crazy if that ever happened to me."

She could tell he really didn't want to talk about it, so she let it drop. "I guess I should take you home pretty soon," he suggested, waiting for Judie to respond one way or another.

"I'd like to stop somewhere first," she said apprehensively. Russ parked the car on a dirt road, and Judie chuckled nervously, saying it was kind of corny—a lover's lane—and had he run out of gas? Russ laughed, too, and moved closer to her. She refused to sit next to him while he drove even though he wanted her to. She couldn't help thinking that Amy probably had.

"Do you want to get in the back seat?" he asked in a Dracula voice, moving his eyebrows up and down as he spoke.

"Sure, why not?" she said, though she didn't move. He opened his car door and got in the back seat. She was glad he didn't climb over.

"It's lonesome back here," he said, still trying to lighten the tension.

She opened her door and got in the back seat with Russ. He kissed her a few times, but then he stopped and asked what was wrong. "Nothing," she said, "at least nothing I can figure out."

He held her a few more minutes and then started kissing her again. For a while, she forgot about whatever it was that was bothering her, but when Russ started to unbutton her blouse, she pulled away. She was thinking of her dream the night before, and she wanted to cry out. She couldn't tell Russ about it and certainly not Tack. It all seemed so overwhelming. "I'm afraid," she said to Russ, and he put her head on his shoulder.

"It's okay," he said, misunderstanding her fear as apprehension about sex, "we don't have to. Maybe it's too soon." He looked at her, then kissed the top of her head and buried his face in her hair.

She was too confused to tell Russ that he misunderstood. Or did he misunderstand? Was she really just afraid to have sex with him? Was that why she thought of the dream?

Soon, Russ suggested they go back to her house and watch TV. On the way there, she felt a lot of frustrations. She had wanted him, she was sure of that. But was it really him she wanted? Did it matter?

Russ left not long after they got there. "I'm sorry," he said as he was leaving. "I hope I didn't screw anything up. I want to see you again soon, okay? You're the only girl I care about." He leaned down and kissed her, more lightly this time. She told him she was sorry she had gotten weird.

"Hokey as it sounds," she said, "I really don't know what came over me." He nodded, told her not to worry, and made his way out the door. She watched Russ through the glass as he backed out of the driveway, just as Tack had done the night before.

Chapter Nineteen

"Hustle over," the coach yelled during Monday's practice. "We've got more than a game this week; we've got our last chance to practice before the state tournament begins. Keep that in mind when you start griping about long practices."

Judie and all the other B-team players only half listened to the coach, since Friday's game would be their last for the season. Judie knew she wouldn't be playing any more varsity ball after the B team lost without her. They needed to win this last game to put them in a tie for second place in the conference. Besides, Bruce Connors's knee hadn't given him any trouble since the rumors of surgery died down.

She had plans to go out with Russ again the following weekend, and he asked if he could start picking her up for school and taking her home. But Judie didn't want him to. Those were the only times she spent with Tack anymore, what with being with Russ at school and on weekends. Though Russ said it had nothing to do with it, Judie was sure he wanted to pick her up just so she couldn't spend any time with Tack.

"I think you're jealous," Judie said one afternoon. She wasn't afraid of making him angry anymore. In fact, sometimes she thought she must try to make him mad, as often as she did it. And, like usual, he got angry just as she anticipated.

"Why would I be jealous of him? I know you're just friends."

"Good," Judie said, "so you'll understand that I want to spend time with my friends, and you won't bother me about our carpooling."

His eyes narrowed into a frown that Judie recognized. "Yeah, I guess," he said. "Besides, Tack doesn't need you. He's got all the girls crawling all over him. I hear the reason he dates so many girls is that he's into one night stands."

"That sounds immature, Russ. Or like a soap opera. Anyway, I'm disappointed in you, and I don't know why you'd say something like that."

They fought that day and any other time the topic of Tack came up. She shared her problems with Tack, but she never told him of this particular difficulty she and Russ had, until later that week when he drove up right after she'd just gotten off the phone with Russ, and they'd been fighting.

"He just refuses to tolerate my relationship with you," she said. "He just stops listening if I mention your name."

Tack smiled. "I love it," he said, "and I can't help it. I just love the thought of him being jealous." Judie thought he looked especially cute sitting there in his car, his hair tousled from the wind.

She tried to find out why he loved it so much that Russ was jealous, but he changed the subject, and she let it drop. "So why'd you drop by if you're going to ignore me?" she asked.

His eyes got big. "The coach told me that he thought I'd be starting this week," Tack exclaimed.

"Great!" Judie yelled. She leaned into the open car window and hugged his neck. "Congratulations, Tack.

That's great. I don't know how to tell you how happy I am for you."

"So can I take you for a celebratory hamburger tonight?" he asked.

"Sure," she said, "as long as Mom doesn't care. I'll go see." Judie left knowing Russ would call back before she returned home.

"Tonight's been so much fun," Tack said while they were waiting for their hamburgers. "It's been like...like B.R."

"B.R.?" Judie asked.

"Before Russ," he said, presenting that lopsided grin he smiled when he was being a bit sarcastic.

Judie felt a little sad, especially since she felt the same way as Tack. She missed spending evenings with him. Things with Russ were good, she thought, but she couldn't help wondering if she should spend less time with Russ so she could spend more with Tack. Maybe if she could get Russ to see she should spend more time with her friends, it could work out. But she knew if Russ ever pressed her about her feelings about Tack, some of his suspicions would be confirmed.

"Earth to Judie," Tack said, snapping his fingers in front of her face. "Come in, Judie," he said in a piercing monotone.

"You never change," she said wistfully, as though they'd been apart for years.

"This isn't our twenty-fifth class reunion, you know. Are you okay?" he asked, his face taking on a look of concern.

"Sure, I'm okay."

"Are you happy?"

She hesitated. "Yeah. I think I'm happy."

"You're either happy or you're not happy."

"Then I'm happy," she said, stirring her Coke with her straw, "but only because I'm not unhappy."

Tack shifted in his seat. "Well, I'm not that happy, myself. I guess I miss you."

"I miss you, too, Tack. But I don't know what I can do about it."

"I guess that's something only you can decide," he said formally.

"But I don't know what I'm deciding about, Tack. I don't know what I feel right now. I don't seem to know anything." She put her head in her hands. "Do you ever dread getting older? Getting more problems?"

"Sure," he said, "but I don't think I have any more or less problems than I've had in the past or I'll have in the future. But changing does hurt some." His face looked unbelievably vulnerable and Judie wanted very much to reach across the table and touch him with her hand, feel his soft skin, wipe away that hurt look.

But she didn't. "Cheer up, Tack. This is a celebratory hamburger, after all."

"Number 67," the burly waiter yelled. Judie looked around. They were the only people in the place. Tack did the same.

"Did he just pick that number out of a hat or what?" Tack asked in a whisper.

"It's his favorite number," Judie teased. Tack was still snickering when he got up to pick up their order.

When Judie got home that night, her mother told her that Russ had called twice. Judie didn't return his calls; she didn't want to talk to him. The next day at school, he didn't come by her locker as he usually did, and during practice, they avoided each other completely.

Finally, after the scrimmage, Russ walked over to her and asked if he could take her home. She agreed, then told Tack not to wait. It was odd when she and Russ were fighting; everyone at practice could tell. Once, when Russ fouled out of the scrimmage, the coach yelled "What's wrong with you today, Dwyer?"

Franky chimed in, "Marital problems, Coach," and everyone laughed, even the coach.

"I want to talk to you and Judie after practice," the coach said to Franky.

"I promise, Coach," Franky said, "I haven't laid a hand on her." This time, even Judie laughed.

After most of the players had entered the showers, the coach told Judie and Franky that they were going to be traveling with the varsity to the state tournament. Friday's game was their "in"—if they won, they automatically went to quarterfinals, and with their perfect record, they should be seeded first, and likely they would draw a bye, sending them straight to the semifinal round. "And it's likely we'll be without Bruce. Tack will be the number-two guard, leaving you two for subs."

Franky looked at Judie quizzically. "That's all," the coach said, getting up and leaving the two in the middle of the empty gym.

"That scare you any?" Franky asked.

"Yes," she said, waiting for a smart remark.

"Me, too," he said, leaving her at the locker room door.

128

Chapter Twenty

"I don't see any really good reason why you should go," Russ said. "That's the weekend I wanted us to go visit my father in Kansas City. He wants to meet you."

"That's the first time I've heard about getting invited to see your father that weekend," Judie said hotly. "Pretty convenient, if you ask me."

He jumped up and walked across the living room. His mother was away for the weekend, and instead of going to the movies like she told her parents, she and Russ went to his house.

"But you won't get to play, you know. Last night, you didn't even get to suit up for the varsity. The last B-team game, and you played all four quarters."

"The coach just wants some depth for the state tournament. He said today that Bruce definitely won't be playing."

"Where did you see the coach today?" Russ asked, his face red with anger.

"We had a special practice this morning," Judie said, wishing she'd told him earlier so it wouldn't seem as though she'd kept it from him on purpose.

"Wonderful. I'm glad you made up your mind before talking to me."

"What's to talk about?" she yelled. "I've been asked to travel with the varsity, and I'm going to. You would."

"Franky is enough depth. Anyway, with Bruce gone and Tack playing, we don't stand a chance anyway."

"That's ridiculous," Judie said, trying to calm down. His acting like a child was no reason for her to act the same way. "I think you're just jealous," she said in an even voice.

"Why don't you just leave, then, if that's what you think."

"Fine," Judie said, "that sounds like the smartest thing you've said all night."

"And make sure you run and tell Tack all about tonight. I'm sure he'll love it," he said sarcastically, in a softer voice. They were facing each other, not more than three feet apart.

Judie wanted to cry out that she'd be happy to go to Tack, that Tack was at least happy for her, but she didn't want to play his games any more. She simply turned and left him standing there, his chin jutted out in anger. She didn't want to fight about it, and she wasn't willing to confuse the issue.

She walked to a phone booth, and, once there, she had to decide who to call. She didn't want to call her parents. She'd have to explain why she wasn't at the movies, and then why she'd left Russ. She didn't want them to be as angry with her as Russ was—their anger wouldn't be easily forgotten. And anyway, this was her problem, not theirs.

It was too far to walk home. Better call Tack, she reasoned. Call him and tell him everything right now. Make him feel miserable for you. Have him comfort you. Make it all feel better somehow.

Judie reached into her pocket to see how much money she had. Enough for a cab and the phone call to get one here, she thought. It wasn't Tack's problem, seeing him would only cloud the issues. She put the money in the slot and called a taxi. It would be dark soon.

The team practiced nonstop from three thirty to six thirty daily after school, and then after dinner, Tack went to Judie's house to play some more, or the two of them went to the Rec Center for a game. It was Grayson who suggested that they not leave the gym so early; he wanted to practice until six thirty, go eat dinner as a team, and reassemble for more scrimmages at seven thirty. "That way we can play as a team more," he pleaded to the coach. "We all go somewhere to practice later in the evening anyway."

The coach surveyed the group. He knew Grayson had the discipline, but did the others? The only hesitation came from the reserve center. "We practice enough already," he said, sure he would get other support once someone had spoken.

Grayson glared at him. It was the first time anyone had seen him really show anger. "Then get out of here, Dalton. We don't need you."

"Settle down, Grayson," the coach said. "Any others who don't want to?" He looked at all twelve players. "Speak now if you're going to."

No one moved. The next night, Wednesday, they began playing more and more. The coach had used his twelve-player limit wisely, Judie thought. Five guards, five forwards, and two centers. Enough players so that at least the guards and forwards get to rest occasionally during practice. But with Bruce not playing because of his knee, Judie rarely got a chance to rest. Both Wednesday and Thursday night, Judie got home around ten-thirty and collapsed in her bed without even taking her clothes off. She had never talked to Russ on the phone since the fight, and except for simple courtesy

131

conversations at school, they never talked at all. And she was too damned busy to call him this week—not that she would anyway.

Tack laughed at her plight when she explained it. "You were absolutely right, of course, about his being jealous of you." Judie didn't mention that she had walked out on Russ during a conversation about Tack, or that she had wanted to call him to take her home. But she was glad that he agreed with her, though she never doubted that he would.

But his words surprised her. "I don't see why you hang around him at all—he's such a jerk. A complete asshole, if you ask me." Judie stared at him. Though she suspected that he wasn't crazy about Russ, he'd never before said anything against him. Tack returned her stare. "I just don't see what you see in him. But it's your life, and there's no accounting for tastes—or lack of."

"I don't care what you think of Russ, so keep it to yourself," she said sharply.

"Fine," he said sarcastically, nodding his head up and down. He looked out the passenger window as Judie drove on to his house, the tension unbearable.

Judie pulled into Tack's driveway and left the car running to indicate that she wasn't staying. Tack looked at her. She could tell she'd really hurt his feelings. "I'll see you tomorrow morning, Judie," he said sweetly. "Try to get some sleep tonight."

He reached for the door handle, and Judie touched his arm before he got out of the car. "I'm sorry," she said.

He shook his head "no." "You didn't do anything wrong. It was lousy of me to say that about Russ—he's your boyfriend. I don't have any right to do that."

"Yes, you do," Judie pleaded. "I love you," then realizing what she'd said, she quickly tried to cover up her slip. "I mean you're my best friend and I care about what you think. Your opinion matters a lot." She stopped talking, and without looking at Tack, put the car in reverse. She knew he must still be looking at her because he hadn't shut the car door. Finally, their eyes met, but they looked away quickly, and he shut the door. Judie backed out of the driveway without waiting to see him go inside. She knew her face was bright red, and she didn't want him to see her so embarrassed. She wished she'd been able to see his reaction more clearly. Her own feelings were so overwhelming that all she could remember from his glance was that she'd never seen such a look on Tack's face before. Her heart pounded all the way home.

The bus was leaving for Dolene, the tournament site, at seven thirty Friday morning. They didn't play until Saturday afternoon, but the coach didn't want them to have a long bus ride before the game. It had been a long time since Meier had made it to the State Semifinals, and they were going in style.

Judie's mother told her before she left that she and her father were driving up for the game Saturday morning. "And we're getting hotel reservations so we can see the finals game that night."

The other semifinal round was Friday night, and once they watched the game, they would know what to look for in the finals round, should they win. Meier was seeded first, and as a result, had drawn a bye in the quarterfinal round as the coach had expected. But that had its disadvantages, he explained. All the other teams had played good competition in their quarters rounds, and had won. Meier had not played since the regional game.

Oddly enough, the fourth seeded team was the team the coach had spotted early in the season as "the team to beat." Due to some freak occurrence, they had lost two games during their regular season, and their record put them in the fourth position in the state listings. As a result, Meier was scheduled to play them, the Madison Tigers, in the state semifinal round, making the game what sports writers statewide called the "the real state championship."

Chapter Twenty-one

Spirits were high on the bus that morning, and everyone told jokes and stories; Franky was even nice to Judie. Only Grayson sat by himself in the front of the bus, looking at a profile a local newspaper had done about the opposition.

It was Tack, finally, who asked Grayson to come back and give them a little insight about the other team.

"Do you really want me to?" he asked. "I've been such a bear all week. It's just so important to me."

"We'd like to hear," Judie piped up, and everyone voiced support.

"Our main problem isn't height, for once," he began, his face intense, his knuckles tight around the rolled-up newspaper. "Their big man, Clark Jones, is only 6'5". Anthony is 6'6". Boyd's as tall as Jones. Their tallest forward is a kid by the name of Ron Wood, and he's only 6'3". Just a little taller than I am." He tapped the paper rhythmically on his palm, stared at the aisle floor, and paused before each word, making it sound incredibly ominous to everyone.

"No, our problem isn't going to be height. It's speed. They're faster than anyone we've played. According to the stats, they're the number-one team in terms of total points scored. They have one excellent guard, Terry White, and he hasn't left a single game for even so much as a second all year long. We'll have to find a way to be quicker than they are. We'll have to curb their fast break. Mostly, though, we'll have to keep our cool. Fast breaks are murder on our team fouls. Especially you, Anthony. I've heard that Jones is pretty physical under the basket. If you let him get to you, he'll sucker you into fouling out. We can't have that. Boyd, Wood will be yours. He's an extremely good shot from the top of the key and from the left corner of the court. Terry White will be mine. He's the master mind behind their timing." He didn't say another word, and everyone stared at him as he sat trancelike, thinking about the game.

"I feel like I'm getting ready for the bar exam," Tack whispered to Judie after a few silent moments had passed.

"All right, everyone," Franky yelled, jumping out of his seat. "Let's have a little pre-game fun."

"Sit down," Boyd said, usually the first one for fun and games, "I'm concentrating."

Franky made his way over to Tack and Judie. "Looks like a fella has to go see Punch and Judie if he wants a little conversation," he said.

"No, you don't," Tack said. "We're talking."

Franky looked at Tack, who moved closer to Judie. "Hey, Boyd," Franky yelled, "you better start taking notes for your buddy, because this bus is beginning to look like Peyton Place."

"Shut up, Franky," Boyd yelled from the back of the bus.

"I'm telling you, Boyd," Franky said. "One look into the eyes of those two," pointing to Tack and Judie, "and you'll see white lace and promises."

"A kiss for luck and they're on their way...." Pete Dalton said, then he began to hum the tune of "We've

Only Just Begun," and before long, there were enough singers to make a small choir. Before long, Tack started singing along, then Judie joined in, the lone alto voice in the group that sang a little off key, but always good-naturedly, across the state, stopping only when the bus stopped for gas, and not always even then.

As they reached the hotel, the team laughed and joked around just as they'd done on the bus. The coach went into the office and came back with several keys. "The rooms each have two double beds, and..."

"I'm sleeping with Judie," Franky said.

The coach ignored him. "Two rooms will have four guys each. One will have only three," he said, then, turning to Judie, he handed her a key. "You've got a single room on the far west end of the hall."

"Where are you going to be, Coach?" Franky asked.

"Not far enough away from you, Franky," the coach said dryly.

The players each grabbed their respective bags, and when Judie was getting hers, the coach asked her to stay on the bus after the others had gone.

"I'm not sure about using you during tomorrow's game," he said. "Vance says our eligibility will be threatened if you play, but you know Vance. I checked with the State Activities Association, and they just suggested that I not use you. But they couldn't find any specific reason or rule that precludes you from playing. Seems they worded the eligibility section in terms of 'any high school sophomore, junior, or senior is eligible for the tournament provided he had a grade average of blah-blah.' I checked with them about the use of the word 'he' but since they claim it's generic earlier in the code, then I don't see how they could claim otherwise here. I made sure they noted my inquiry and that I was not officially instructed not to use you."

"Then what's the problem?" Judie asked.

"Well," he began, "that crowd is going to be murder if you play. It's the Boys' State Tournament, after all. You might see harassment like you've never seen before. And not just from the crowd. The officials might come down a little hard on you, too."

"What are you saying, Coach? That you don't think I can handle it?"

"Don't get me wrong, Judie, I'd like very much to see you play here. I think every high school ball player should get that chance. And you especially, in light of the kind of crap you've had to take all season long."

Judie looked at the coach appreciatively, fighting back her emotions.

"I'm not blind," he continued. "You've been through a lot and you stuck it out. Most of the boys on the varsity wouldn't have been able to handle that." The coach was turning a little red as he spoke, but he quickly regained his rough exterior. "You wouldn't be here if you didn't deserve it. You're a damned good guard. Especially for someone your height. In fact, I've had qualms about leaving you on the B team, and it was either you or Tack, but he's a little taller and had had more experience with the caliber of our competition. But tomorrow, Judie, we're going to need a third guard and in all likelihood, I'll probably use Franky."

"That's kind of lousy," Judie said, though not very forcefully.

"If this was your senior year or if I didn't think you and Tack could bring this team back next year, I'd use you. But I want to make sure you don't get a lot of unnecessary pressure."

"What if I *want* to play?" Judie asked. "What if I can

see for myself the kind of hostilities from the crowd and all that I'm up against, and I still want to play?"

"We'll see, Judie. I promise I won't put you in unless you agree to it. And I won't tell the others. It will look like my decision."

The coach got off the bus, and Judie watched him walk away carrying his "Meier Mavericks" gym bag and his suit bag, and slinging a Meier sweat jacket from seasons gone by over his arm. Judie sat there on the empty bus and knew for the first time that she absolutely deserved to be there. The coach said she was a good player—"a damned good guard." She day-dreamed about her senior year, about herself and Tack working together on court, and it made her smile.

Chapter Twenty-two

"Let's get some grub," Tack said over the phone. "Meet you in the hotel lobby in fifteen minutes, okay?"

"Okay," she said, tossing her baggage on her twin bed. "I'll be there." She almost forgot her key as she left.

"Is the single room as bad as the sleeps-four version? Do you have black velvet paintings of bull fighters and bandits?" Tack asked as soon as she reached the lobby.

Judie laughed. "You don't have paintings like that!"

"We do, too. Honest."

"I don't believe you," she said.

"After we eat, I'll show you," he said. "Pretty smooth maneuver to get you to my room, huh?"

"Where'd you learn that? *Love American Style* reruns?" she asked. Sometimes even Tack was corny. "Besides if we wanted privacy, it would be stupid to go to your room. You have three roommates." Tack leered at Judie playfully. "That's not necessarily an invitation for titillating and exhausting sexual acts," she retorted.

"But there remains a chance?" he asked, half seriously, knowing he'd better stop before he embarrassed both Judie and himself.

"Excuse me," a deep voice said. They looked up. "My name is Duke Avery. I'm a representative of State University. I'm here to watch you play ball tomorrow," he said, smiling as though he intended to show off every one of his perfectly straight, white teeth. He extended his hand. Tack shook it, then Judie did.

"Aren't you both guards for Meier?" he asked.

Tack and Judie looked at each other. "Yes," Tack said, "but I think you're looking for a different guard. His name is Grayson Griffin." He turned to Judie. "What's his room number?" Tack asked, "Two thirty-four?"

"Two thirty-six, I think," Judie answered.

Duke Avery smiled, then said, "No, I'm not interested in Grayson. There's another, well, another representative speaking with him. I'd like to talk to you about our women's program, Judie. May I call you Judie?"

"Sure," Judie replied, totally confused.

"Judie, women's basketball programs are growing. They're bringing in more revenue year after year. As a result, large schools, schools like State, like to keep up their image as a powerhouse athletic institution in every regard, and so more money is being earmarked for recruiting young women to play. Young women like yourself."

"But I'm only a junior," she said, "and I have another year left."

"I know that. State knows that. But I'm here to get the jump on other schools. Judie, you're going to get a lot of offers from various schools if you play your cards right. You've drawn a lot of attention to yourself by playing on the boys' team. It was a smart move. But I think, and State thinks, that in order to prove how successful you can be in college ball almost requires that you play against other young women during your senior year. What I'm saying is that if you play on the girls' team next year, and if you do as well as we think you will, then you can count on a very attractive offer from State to start college."

"Why should she play on the girls' team if she wants to play on the boys' team? Everyone can see how good she is," Tack said.

"Son," he began, "it all amounts to whether Judie can prove to State that she is as dedicated to basketball as she needs to be. If we request that she play on the girls' team and she does, we can see from her actions that she is dedicated."

"Dedicated to getting a scholarship or dedicated to playing basketball?" Tack said defensively.

"You don't understand," Duke Avery said condescendingly. "Judie needs to play against the very people she is competing against for the scholarships."

"You mean that you want to make sure she's bankable," Tack said.

"Put it however you like," he said to Tack. He turned to face Judie, focusing on her as if Tack had disappeared. "Judie, for scholarships, your mind is made up." He reached into his jacket and pulled out an expensive-looking cigar holder, put a cigar in his mouth, and lit it. "Think about what I said, Judie. I'm sure we'll talk again."

Just then, their food arrived. Duke Avery picked up the check. "Just a hint of how it feels to be wanted," he said, nodding his head. He turned and walked gracefully out the door.

"Cocky son-of-a-bitch, isn't he?" Tack asked, watching the man saunter out of the room.

"Yeah. I wasn't too crazy about him. But I have to admit, the scholarship sounds good."

"Yeah, but you'll get them anyway. Don't worry about what he said. You and I are going to be the best guards in the state next year," he said, shoving the hamburger in his mouth. "We should've ordered steak," Tack said, pointing to the direction Duke Avery just went.

"And champagne," Judie added.

"And a Mercedes sports car."

They laughed, then settled down to eating before getting ready to watch the night's game.

At the gym that night, Judie sat next to Tack. Unlike some states, in her old state it was the rule that the losers of semifinals rounds both be awarded a third-place trophy instead of making them battle for the spot. Judie believed it was a merciful rule; her old state did the opposite, and she could think of little worse than, after just having lost a semi round, to get back on court and fight for an award you never really wanted anyway. Once you weren't playing for the championship, it didn't matter too much if you won or not.

She was reaching into Tack's sack of popcorn when the coach came up to her. "Judie, come here for a minute," he said. She walked down the bleachers with him and tried to keep up with the big steps he was taking. "They want to interview you," he said, pointing to a man in a three-piece gray polyester suit who was standing in front of a camera man.

Judie looked at the coach and began to ask him why they wanted to interview her, when he answered smiling, "You're the maverick of the Mavericks." Judie rolled her eyes. "That's what the guy told me," the coach said. "He wants to interview you, but if you don't want to, just tell him. He did say it will be broadcast over most of the Midwest."

The man in polyester made his way over to Judie and the coach. "I'm Rod Lubner," he said, offering her his hand. Judie shook it firmly. "Just look into the camera as I ask you questions and you'll do just fine."

Rod smiled into the camera, looked back to Judie, and took her by the shoulders to position her opposite him.

"You're on," the camera man said.

"Rod Lubner here at the Boys' State Tournament semifinal round of action. Here with me is not a cheerleader as some of you are likely to suspect, but a player in tomorrow's semifinal round, Ms. Judie Conklin. Judie, what position do you play for Meier High School?"

"Uh, guard," she said, wondering how she'd gotten trapped into doing this. She felt ridiculous.

"And you're a junior, is that right?"

"Right."

"Tell me, Judie, what led you to play for the boys' team? Don't you have a girls' team at Meier? Isn't it a 4A school?"

Even Judie knew that he shouldn't be asking so many questions at once. She didn't know which question to answer first.

"Uh, yes, it's 4A. We do have a girls' team, but I'd rather play on the boys'."

"Why is that?" he asked, shoving the microphone under her chin. Judie didn't know what to say.

"Well," she began, "there are a lot of reasons."

Mr. Lubner waited for her to say more, but she didn't. He ended the interview promptly, and Judie could tell from the strained expression on the coach's face that she was right. She'd looked like an idiot. She was glad her parents and Tack wouldn't see her performance, and as for Russ, she didn't really care.

Chapter Twenty-three

The gym seemed larger than it had the night before, and as Judie jogged in from a utility room the tournament personnel had set up for her to use, she could feel her heart begin to pound in unison with the movement of her legs. It was Grayson who turned and saw her running out to where the boys were already warming up, and he hugged her when she reached him.

He was not his usual self today, either. He had signed a letter of intent to play for State and had accepted a full four-year scholarship. His eyes looked a little watery, and Judie could tell that today, his emotions might influence how he played.

They clapped rhythmically while they jogged around the court doing lay-ups. The crowd was restless; the people moved in and out of the gym lobby like cattle through a chute on market day. But Judie could only hear a constant roar in her ears, and she paid little heed to the opposition and their laughter.

The buzzer sounded and the noise rippled across the floor and echoed in the rafters. The crowd began settling down for the game, and the teams went to their respective benches for last minute instructions. Tack put his arm out to Judie as they approached the bench, and he wished her luck. He looked terribly nervous, and as she told him that he'd do fine, he held up his hands to show her that he was shaking. She put her hand on his back as the coach called out his name for final encouragement.

"Welcome to the Annual Boys' State Basketball Tournament," the speakers blasted. "It is traditional in this, the semifinal round, to introduce each and every member of the very fine and capable teams that have made it this far in the competition." The crowd yelled and cheered, and Judie noticed that even she was clapping her hands with the sound. "Meier has won the toss and will be the home team on the scoreboard this afternoon. The visiting team, the Madison Tigers, will now be introduced."

Judie watched each of the opposition run to place on court. As each of them folded his arms in front of his chest, Judie remembered the lecture Grayson had given them. Terry White, the senior guard, was heavier than she had imagined, but he had the same fiercely confident look that Grayson usually wore.

"And now the Meier High School Mavericks," yelled the announcer, as half the crowd cheered and half booed. It was unusual for a crowd to boo the opposition so early; the excitement level was higher than Judie had ever encountered before. It was as though there was some matter of utmost importance to be settled today, and neither side was willing to give the other an ounce of respect for fear they'd lose some of their own.

The starting five ran to position as their names were called first. Judie's name was yelled into the crowd's response to Tack's name, and as she ran on court, her legs felt like lead. Franky's name, which was called after Judie's, was inaudible due to the mixed reaction to her name, and it had to be called again.

The game started. Judie was seated third down from the end of the bench. She was engrossed in the game

146

from the toss of the jump ball, and it seemed important to her to make note of every move that either guard made, in case she had to play against them. As Grayson brought the ball downcourt, she could feel herself move in every direction Grayson moved. She could feel his rhythm, and oddly enough, she felt he made the wrong move just as Terry White slapped the ball away from him and took it all the way back to score.

From then on, Grayson was different. He was everywhere, slapping at balls, double-teaming, breaking downcourt at every possible chance. Quickly, he earned two fouls.

The coach called a time-out. "Settle down, Grayson. They're wearing you out. Don't fight them; just play basketball."

Tack took the ball out and threw it to Grayson. Grayson slowed down this time, taking Terry White with him as he put the ball in play downcourt. To Tack. To Grayson. To Boyd. Boyd from the top of the key. Basket good.

The game was mechanical. Both teams scored routinely, first one, then back down to the opposite end for the other. There were no mistakes made. It was a perfect basketball game—if you liked ticking bombs. Which team would falter first? It was just a matter of time before the game would explode into the final contest.

Judie was proud of Tack. She knew he felt as though he were the weakest cog in the wheel, but she doubted that Bruce would have been able to do any more than Tack. The opposing guard was taller, but he wasn't as quick as Tack, and Tack used that advantage. It startled him when, in the second quarter, Grayson told him to bring the ball downcourt for the first time.

Was Grayson getting tired? He couldn't be, not with

all the extra practices and running he'd been doing before school just to get in better shape. Terry White seemed fearless; his face never changed expression. Even when Grayson did something outstanding, like make a jump shot twenty feet out, White never responded in the least. Judie thought Grayson might have gone too far, psyched himself out; and with the intimidating looks of Terry White, he seemed to have lost the unshakable confidence that was so important to his game.

Meier lost the ball two times in a row, and Grayson's eyes burned a new light: revenge. He was everywhere like before, but this time was different. He was a one-man show. Scoring, getting rebounds, stealing the ball from Terry White, Grayson moved like a panther. His body felt the move of every other body on court, and he used his instinct to step in at the right moment, take the ball away, and fire the ball downcourt. When he was dribbling, the ball appeared to be attached in some way to his hand. It looked like a yo-yo. He had perfect control.

Then he got his third foul, and he played even more wildly, getting his fourth foul just before the half-time buzzer.

At the coach's insistence, Judie followed the boys into their locker room. "We've got to make them play our pace," he said, while the players concentrated on his every word. During a pause, Judie looked around and saw Grayson, sitting in the corner of the room, head in hands, and her heart went out to him. If they lost, it was his last game, and third place wasn't good enough for Grayson, regardless of the size of his scholarship. As they filed out of the room, Judie read desperation in his face.

"Coach," a voice yelled from the doorway to the gym.

Judie looked and saw Mr. Vance motioning the coach over. She made a point to slow down so she could pass them once they were talking.

"Glad to see you're seeing my point of view about the girl," Mr. Vance said. "Grayson will straighten out, and if he doesn't, that Warnik boy will do fine once the jitters leave."

The coach stared at him. "I haven't made any decisions yet, Vance, and if it so happens that Judie doesn't play, you can be absolutely sure it has nothing to do with you or your suggestions. I'm the coach, and I make the decisions," he said cooly, and turning to walk away, he saw Judie and winked at her.

The coach did put Franky in to relieve some of the pressure on Grayson. But Franky was lost against White, and the coach was forced to put Grayson back in before they got too far behind. It was when Grayson made the tying basket that he came down on White, and was called for charging. Grayson was out of the game, and there was a full quarter left to play.

Franky tried hard to stay with White, but he couldn't, and Tack was no better. With five minutes left, Franky called a time-out. Meier was trailing by eight. "Put Judie in," Franky said.

The coach stared at him, trying to gage his sincerity. He was always setting her up, the coach knew, and he told him "no" without even asking Judie.

"You're making a mistake, Coach," Grayson said finally, his face streaked with sweat and tears. "White is too quick for Franky or Tack. Judie's our only hope of curbing him."

The coach stared at Judie earnestly. If she didn't give him some sort of sign, he wasn't going to put her in and she knew it. When she spoke, her voice was soft but firm. *"I want to play, coach."*

He patted her back, then sent her to the timer's table to report in. The Madison crowd bellowed boos, and then, to Judie's surprise, Meier fans cheered. Make it count, she told herself, her fists balled up tightly. She took her position on court.

Tack threw her the ball, and slowly she maneuvered the ball around White and passed off to Boyd, who was open. Basket good. The crowd roared.

It was her turn to try to keep up with White. He had underestimated her, she knew, and Judie could see a look of renewed determination in his stare. She stayed with him as he inched down the length of the floor. The coach had put them in a full court press, and whenever White moved, Judie moved, too.

He passed off to Wood, the bigger forward. Judie felt good; he hadn't been able to push up the middle as he'd done with Franky. But Madison scored anyway, and Judie knew it would be a struggle to regain the lead.

Tack took the ball downcourt this time, and when he found her open, he passed off. She put up the shot, and it was good, but White slapped her arm trying to block her shot. "One foul shot," the referee yelled.

The teams positioned themselves around the key. Judie looked at Tack, who winked at her and shook his head up and down.

"Rebound!" the Madison fans yelled.

"Come on, Judie," a voice cried out; it sounded like Franky.

Judie stared at the orange rim as it jutted from the glass backboard. "Breathe," she told herself softly. She positioned the ball in her hands, bounced the ball four times—a superstition—and pushed the ball toward the basket. As soon as she felt it leave her fingertips, she knew it was good.

Madison took it out again, and, like before, both

teams were playing perfect ball—no mistakes, no appreciable change between their scores.

With one minute left, the coach called a time-out. "Feed it to Anthony," he said. "And move fast. We don't have any time to spare." Judie didn't think the coach thought they had a chance to regain the five points they lagged behind, but she pressed on anyway.

Judie and Tack moved like twins. She knew his every move and he knew hers. They played well, each of them scoring but neither of them saw an opportunity to hit Anthony under the basket despite the coach's instructions.

Tack took the ball away once, and then, on Madison's next attempt to score, Judie took the ball away. With ten seconds left, Meier trailed by only three points, and the coach called their last time-out.

"Make this basket as quickly as you can, and then foul the shorter forward if you can. But do it quickly, to whoever has the ball, and then pray he misses. Then get your asses down here and score." He put his hand out, and the players put their hands on top of his.

"Let's go!" they yelled in unison, and ran to position. Tack took the ball out of bounds, and Judie tried to shake Terry White. When she did, Tack threw it to her, and she simply outran him down the court, dribbling faster and more smoothly than she ever had, and she felt completely calm. She was going to make this basket, she told herself. And without help from anyone, she found a hole in the Madison defense, and made a lay-up that looked too easy to be believed.

The Meier crowd and the bench jumped to their feet, shouting her name. There were six seconds left on the clock, and she glanced at Tack, then at her other teammates. They all knew to try to catch the shorter forward with the ball if they could; he was the poorest free-throw shooter they had. None of them would foul out, so it was only a matter of who had the best opportunity.

But Madison made sure they kept the ball away from him. Terry White held the ball, dribbled, and refused to put himself in the position to have to throw it to someone else. They were stalling, and if someone had to make a free shot, they wanted it to be White.

With three seconds left, Judie slapped his hand as he was dribbling. The teams made their way to the key, and both sides of the crowd were silent as he began to concentrate. Judie tried not to think about anything besides the game. If only he would miss, Meier could win.

But he didn't miss either shot, and Meier trailed again by three. And with three seconds left, the Madison five knew to stay clear of the Meier team as they took the ball down to score, making sure that no one fouled, which would enable Meier to make a three-point play. When the final buzzer sounded, the score was Madison 86, Meier 85.

Madison fans charged down to the floor to huddle around their team, and Meier fans cleared the stands slowly, sadly, and sorrowfully. Judie let the tears roll down her face freely; she had nothing to be ashamed of. She went over and hugged Tack.

"I feel so bad," he said, as the tears rolled down his face, too. "It was Grayson's last chance. He's worked so hard for this."

Grayson walked over to the two of them. He put his hand out. "Judie," he said, "you did better with Terry White than I did."

Judie started to cry out that she didn't really, that White had just tired, but Grayson shook his head and motioned for her not to speak. "It's true," he said, "you didn't let him get to you. You played your game and not his. And you freaked him out a little bit, I think. He didn't expect you to be so damned good."

"I'm proud of you," the coach said as he walked up to them. "You all did a great job. And any other time, we would have won."

They started to walk to the sidelines when another cameraman and another sports announcer approached them. "Would you like to say a few words, Coach?"

"No, thanks," the coach said.

"How about you, young lady? You were something else out there today."

Judie turned her head away from them, and she grabbed Grayson's arm and Tack's arm. The coach waved the reporters away. "She doesn't want to," he said, "but thanks, anyway."

Tack and Grayson went into the locker room to shower and get ready for the bus ride home, and as Judie started walking to her little room without a shower, the coach took her arm.

"I'm sorry I didn't put you in earlier, Judie," he said. "You could've won the game for us if you'd had the time."

"That might not be true, Coach. You know that sometimes it just doesn't work out that way. But thanks for telling me."

"Tack told me about the scout. He says you're thinking about playing for the girls' team next year."

Judie looked down. She didn't know what to say.

"It's going to be a hard decision to make, I imagine," he said, "but I want you to know that I would hate to lose you. You've proven today that you're one of the best junior guards in the state—boy or girl. And with Grayson leaving, we sure could use a team leader. If we do lose you to the girls' team, we'd be losing more than just a good ball player, that's for sure."

Judie couldn't look at him. She went into her dressing room and wet a towel to try to cool off before she put on her jeans and T-shirt. After she had gotten about halfway dressed, she sat down on the little stool they had provided, and she cried in heaving sobs. Sitting there in the little room, it was hard for her to think about anything beyond how it felt to look at Grayson.

She finished dressing and put her uniform in the gym bag, then walked back out into the gym to find the others. To her surprise, Terry White was standing outside her door.

He offered his hand and she shook it. "Congratulations," she said.

"Thank you," he said in a voice much softer than what Judie imagined him to have. "It's hard to play as well as you did and still lose," he said, "and I just wanted to tell you that it's too bad this was only a semifinal round. You're the best team we've ever played."

Without waiting for any kind of response, he turned and walked away. Judie leaned against the wall and watched him ignore the masses of people trying to shake his hand. In the arena packed with people, Judie watched him hunt until he found Grayson. When Judie saw them shaking hands, she knew that it didn't matter so much that they'd lost, because if Meier had won, it would've been Terry White who bore the same grievous look that Grayson was now wearing.

Chapter Twenty-four

The bus ride home was a quiet one. Judie sat next to the window about halfway back in the bus, and Tack sat with her. Several of the players were lying on the seats, their long bodies either dangling out into the aisle, or if there was no one in the seat across from them, they draped their bodies over the aisle and into the seat directly opposite them.

Judie's body ached, and she had a slight headache from the tension. Tack squirmed in his seat; he didn't have anything to rest against, and Judie knew he just wanted to sit with her so they could be together. She reached over and put his arm around her. "Lean on me," she said, and before long she could tell he was asleep.

It didn't seem odd to Judie to have Tack's face so close to hers even though it was really the first time she'd ever held him. She felt good having him near, and before long, she was asleep, too.

When the bus finally pulled over to get gas, she and Tack woke up. They were lying down across the seats like the other players, but their bodies were intertwined, keeping each other from falling off the narrow seats.

They unfolded from each other quickly, and got off the bus to get something to eat and drink. When they got back on, Tack asked if she'd rather he got a seat of his own.

"Only if you'd be more comfortable," she said, "but I really don't mind the way we were."

Tack sat down with Judie. "I've got a pillow in my bag," he said, getting up to get it. "I always carry my own pillow. I'm a real baby about it. I can't sleep with any other."

Judie smiled at him fondly. Most guys or girls would be too proud to say they needed a certain pillow, but not Tack. "It's my security pillow," he said.

Though they didn't lie back down, they held each other close the rest of the way home. When the bus reached the school parking lot, Judie peered out the window and saw Russ's car parked there, waiting. Waiting for Boyd? For her? She couldn't decide.

When she got off the bus carrying her bags, Russ got out of his car and walked up to her. "I saw you on TV," he said. "You looked very pretty."

She sat her bags down on the asphalt. Why did Russ have to comment on her looks now? Talk about bad timing.... "A college scout approached me when I was there," she said flatly. "He told me that if I wanted to prove that I was bankable, I should play on the girls' team next year. He said I'd get some pretty good scholarships that way."

"That sounds smart," Russ said, picking up her bags. She followed him and her bags to his car. "You'd be incredible on the girls' team. The best in the state, I bet."

"Russ, do you really think I should play on the girls' team? I'd really like playing on the boys'. I'm sure I'd get to start."

"I wouldn't be so sure," Russ said. "And besides, it would be so much easier on you to play for the girls' team. Not to mention more profitable." He looked over at her, then took her in his arms. "I'd like you to play for the girls' team, Judie."

She pulled away. "I already have a ride home, Russ. I told Tack I'd ride with him." She picked up her bags and started walking back to the bus.

"Why are you riding home with him? I haven't seen you in a long time," Russ said. "I'm sorry I was a jerk about this weekend, but I wanted you to meet my dad and everything...."

Judie wasn't sure Tack was still around, but she walked on anyway. She wasn't sure how Tack felt about her, but it was time she stopped hiding her feelings. Even if he was gone, and even if he didn't care about her the way she hoped, staying with Russ was not what she wanted.

Tack was sitting on his suitcase next to his car, and his hands were shoved deep in his coat pockets. "Need a ride?" he asked.

Russ was still standing behind her. "Judie," he said, "come with me." His black eyes danced with anger, but Judie returned his stare without flinching.

"I'd rather ride with Tack."

Russ turned to walk away, but as he did, he said, "If that's the way you want it, okay. But if you do, it's over between us, Judie."

"Then it's over, Russ.... Ready to go, Tack?"

"Ready as ever." He winked.

Judie put her bags in the car, wondering if she were right about Tack. Like always, she worried about the possibility of ruining their friendship. If he felt differently than she did...

"So, which team are you going to play for next year?"

"Well, it is a tough decision," she said, "and Russ told me I'd be crazy not to play for the girls' team."

"Dumb bastard," Tack said. "You know you'd be a quitter if you didn't play for the boys' team. Playing for the girls' team is the easy way out."

Judie sat in silence. She didn't want to go home yet, though she'd be happy to talk to her parents. She figured they would want her to play on the girls' team, too, but it didn't really matter what anyone else thought.

"Can I pull over somewhere?" he asked. "So we can talk?"

"Good idea," she said.

Tack drove out of town down a winding country road. He parked the Mustang next to a fence row on the crest of a little hill.

"You have to play for the boys' team, Jude," he said pleadingly.

"Why?" she asked.

"Because I want you to and because you want to. If you really don't want to, then I don't want you to. But I think you do."

"I have already decided to play on the boys' team. It's been unfair of me to keep asking you and Russ what you think, making you feel like I'm unsure. The fact of the matter is that I don't care how easy playing for the girls' team is, or how big the scholarship might be, I can't leave this team. I love it, and there's really no other decision I could make."

She looked at him, and he leaned over the stick shift lever and gave her a hug. "Congratulations," he said, "you made the right choice."

"You and the coach are the only two who think so," she said defensively.

"I doubt that. The guys were really impressed with you today. Like it or not, they don't want to lose Meier's number-one junior guard."

She knew it was hard for him to say that. "Tack," she began.

"Shh," he said, "you don't have to respond to that. Besides, I want to talk about more important things."

"Like?" Judie asked, her heart pounding.

"Like," he said, looking out his window to the dark field, "like I'm crazy about you, and I have been for a long time. You're my best friend, and I don't want to mess that up, but I want more."

"I do, too," Judie said. "But we'll have to be careful. It's so much, so big, that I really don't know how to deal with it."

"I thought for a long time that you've felt like I do. Several times I almost said something, but I really thought you cared for Russ."

"I did care for Russ, and I still do, sort of. But it wasn't ever like what I feel for you."

"It will be tough, you know? We know each other so damned well that we can recognize any little game the other plays."

"Maybe we won't have to play any games."

He leaned over the lever again and kissed her. "I think I love you, Jude."

"Pretty heavy stuff for a first date."

"Yeah, it is," he said, smiling the slow smile that kind of took over his whole face.

"I don't know if I'm ready for it," Judie said honestly, turning to him, suddenly shy.

"I don't know if I am either, but I want to try."

"So do I," Judie whispered, reaching to hold him close—*"I want to try."*